WATCH ME
land

WATCH ME
Land

C.E. JOHNSON

Cover design: Jena Brignola
Editor: Sandra Dee, One Love Editing

This book is for you.
You've been through a lot the past year and a half.
Never forget to breathe, give yourself grace, and know tomorrow
is a brand new day.

CHAPTER ONE

MASON

GILL PASSES ME A GLASS, and I dump the dark amber liquid down my throat. It's boys' weekend at the lodge, and I plan on getting shitfaced enough that I forget all about the last time I was here. I've managed to keep my mind occupied with anything other than that dance between Andi and me at Lucas and Tana's wedding two months ago. Having her in my arms did something to me. And I don't fucking like it.

"Listen, brother," Everest says, smacking the back of my shoulder and taking the seat next to me. "If you're going to be shootin' it down like that, just take the damn bottle." He slides the bottle closer to me, and Gill grabs a beer out of the cooler on the ground next to him.

The sliding door at the back of Gill's house opens, and Lucas walks out with a tray of food. "Don't tell him that. I ain't carrying his ass all the way back to his camper." He sets the food down on the table and sits across from me. Coming down here was a great reason to bust out the new camper I bought.

I still can't believe I'm here. Gill and Everest weren't my biggest fans when we were in prison together. Truth be told, I hated everyone for a long time and made it known. But they got out before Lucas and I did. That extra time the two of us had together in that hellhole opened my eyes that just maybe everyone on earth wasn't out to get me. That it was still possible for good people to exist. I got myself into a bind in there with a few really bad dudes, and Lucas stood up for me. I might have died in that fight, and at that time, I really didn't care. But Lucas wasn't having it. And now, not only do I have one brother in this world, I have three.

After helping Lucas save Tana, Gill and Everest brought me inside what they call their circle. Even though it's only been a few months, it feels like we've been brothers forever.

"You guys need anything else?" Natalie, Gill's wife, asks through the door. "I'm going to head to Melanie's house."

"You already did too much. Go put your feet up," Lucas says. With these guys, the bond goes so much deeper than just with each other. Their women became family too.

Gill gets up from his chair and pulls Natalie into his arms, placing a hand on her protruding pregnant belly. "Have fun, Blue. Text me when you get there, and tell my sister to chill on the baby gifts. That room is going to be too full to put the baby in soon."

"If you think telling her that is going to stop her, you're wrong. Bye, guys, have fun. But not so much that I come home to four guys passed out on the lawn," she says, grinning.

"Every party has a pooper, and the pooper is you," Lucas sings to her, and she giggles, then walks back into the house as we wave goodbye.

"What's going on with the diner?" Gill asks Lucas. "I can't believe you haven't talked Tana into working for you yet."

"I don't want to talk her into it. She doesn't have to work at all, but she likes the diner. I don't think she'll ever quit as long as Andi owns it."

Everest leans his elbows onto the table. "That finally go through?" he asks. But now, he's looking at me.

"How would I know?"

"You tellin' me you haven't talked to Andi at all since the wedding?"

Fuck. "Nah, it's been a while." *Eight weeks, three days, and about nineteen hours, to be exact.* Not like I'm paying attention. Not like she's gotten in my head. Not like she's different.

"That's a damn shame," Gill says. "I thought you two…"

"You thought wrong," I interrupt, grabbing the bottle, putting it to my mouth, and pouring some of its contents in.

I look around the table at the three men who just went dead silent with a look I don't care for on their faces, complete with matching grins.

This is that brotherhood Lucas told me stories about every day as we worked together on the roofs. The type where they know you better than anyone else and don't hesitate to tell you like it is. Looking around this table, I know I'm officially in it.

"I still can't believe you ditched having lunch with me at the diner to eat cold, shitty sandwiches in your car," Lucas says. "Even Tana doesn't know what the hell went on with you two. Obviously something if neither of you are talking. So why don't you spill. Maybe we can help you out."

"Nothing happened."

Gill squints at me over the table. "Nothing?"

"I swear it. Nothing happened. We danced, had a few drinks, I walked her to her cabin, and I went to mine. That was it."

"Then I guess you won't have a problem with coming to the diner on Tuesday with me." Lucas grabs a piece of cheese from the board, shoves it in his mouth, and leans back in his chair, looking all sorts of happy with himself for putting me on the spot. I'm kind of glad he's doing it though. I can't avoid her forever. Especially with how close I am with Lucas and Tana. She's bound to be around, and I have missed the diner's patty melt.

"Nope. No problem at all." A rush of uncertainty rages inside, and I grab the bottle and take another swig. *Damn.*

———

I WAS REALLY HOPING the last three days would go by at a snail's pace and maybe Lucas would forget all about dragging me with him to the diner. But boys' weekend flew by, and yesterday we started and finished a small roof all in one day. A roof we had scheduled two days for. Instead, we worked until the sun was nearly setting. That's the benefit of working directly with the owner. He can make those decisions so we can have days like today where we have a lot of spare time. But that's also the downfall of today. We have a lot of spare time. To sit. In this diner.

Tana flashes us a wide smile as we walk in the door. "Sit wherever," she says as she passes us with a huge tray filled with plates of food. I follow Lucas to the furthest booth in the corner and sit with my back facing the kitchen. I want to be inconspicuous, but I also can't help but eye around the diner, keeping a lookout for Andi.

"Hey, guys," Tana says, walking up to the table and setting down two glasses of ice water. She takes a deep breath and exhales loudly as she pulls out her little notepad and pen.

"You okay?" Lucas asks, and I'm all ears. If she says anything other than yes, there are two men sitting in this booth that will have a big problem with that. "I'm fine." She puts her hand on his shoulder, and I watch them fall back to a relaxed position. "But I'm not sure Andi is going to survive today. The poor thing."

"What do you mean?" I ask, my shoulders now the ones that have tensed.

"Brice had to leave. His mom got sick or something, so he rushed out of here."

"What about the other two waitresses?"

"Jessica and Rhonda took vacation, and they're out of town together. Andi thought since we close at five now, the four of us could handle it. But without Brice, Andi is the only one back there cooking, I'm running like crazy, and of course, we've been busy all day."

"Excuse me? Miss?" I follow Lucas's eyes to a man sitting behind me, a few tables away.

"I'll be right back."

Neither of us takes our eyes off the older man as he shoves his plate back at her and points at the hamburger. She walks into the back, and I turn back around in my seat. Lucas, however, still hasn't stopped murdering the man with his eyes as he glares over my shoulder. A minute later, his eyes narrow again, and I know Tana probably just came into view. Only once I turn around, it's not Tana at the table. Andi places the plate back in front of the man, and I read her lips apologizing to him.

She turns to walk back into the kitchen, but I can't stop watching her or wishing I got a better view of her entire face. I get my wish as she looks back once more before she walks through the swinging door and she locks her drained, teary eyes on me. I can't watch this. When I turn back to Lucas, his focus is on my face, reading me like a damn autobiography.

"What do we have left to do today?" I ask.

"Go."

"You sure?"

"If you think for one second I'm okay with that look on her face, you're out of your mind."

My heart beats a little faster as I slide out of the booth. As I'm walking across the dining room, Tana comes barreling out of the back kitchen with another tray. She gives me an apologetic look and stops next to me.

"I'm sorry. I'm sure you two are hungry. I'll be right over, I swear."

"I worked in a fast-food restaurant when I was a teenager. I know it's not the same, but it's something."

Just like her husband, Tana's lips turn up. It's like every damn page is wide open. She winks at me as she leaves my side and delivers her tray of food to a table.

I slowly push open the swinging door. Andi stands at the end of a long stainless steel counter, her hands shoulder-width apart, her head bowed down between them. One loud sniff is all it takes for me to move to her.

"Hey." I roll up my sleeves and wash my hands in the sink. "Show me where everything is."

Her head jolts up, the tears streaming down her cheeks. *Shit.* I knew she was upset and stressed-out, but I didn't think she would be back here crying this hard.

"What are you doing?" she asks, standing upright.

"I can help you. Lucas and I are done for the day, which means point me in the direction you need me."

"Did Tana ask you to do this?"

I dry my hands and stand in front of her as she stares at me. "No."

"Lucas?"

"Nope."

"Then why are you doing this? I thought you hated me."

Tana peeks through the small window from the waitress area and puts another order ticket up. "They just keep coming, girl. I'm sorry," she says and then disappears again.

"Hated you? What the hell gave you that impression?"

She crosses her arms over her chest. "Oh, I don't know.

Maybe because the sweet guy I came to know after months of coming into this diner with Lucas suddenly disappeared after spending only a few hours with me. I must have done something to repel you." She wipes the tears from her cheeks with the back of her hand and rips the order from where Tana pinned it up.

She huffs, opens the door to the walk-in cooler, and steps inside. Fighting my own fucked-up brain to come up with something to say, I wait for her to come back out. Only when she does, I still can't give her a reason. A tub of chicken salad makes a thud as she drops it onto the counter.

"What the fuck was I thinking? I've never owned a restaurant before. What if I can't do this?"

Judging by the tone and volume of her voice, I'd be willing to bet she was asking those questions to herself. But they sure were loud enough for me to hear.

"Yeah? I didn't know the first thing about putting on a roof either. I learned. And you'll learn how to make this place run like nobody else could. Today might suck." She angles her eyes at me. "Okay, it *does* suck. That doesn't mean tomorrow will. You know how I know you're going to make it?"

"How?"

"Every employee you have loves you. Tana doesn't have to work another day in her damn life. But she chooses to stay here and work with you. You're a great boss. And a great friend."

Her chest rises and falls as her eyes bore into me, and Tana places another ticket up. She plucks it from the line and slowly holds it up in my direction. "Thank you."

I thought spending an evening with Andi was difficult. Working alongside her is like running into a wall face-first over and over again. The stress on her face lifted as the day went on. A few of my jokes even managed to make her laugh out loud. She bounced between helping Tana wait the tables, answering the phones, and occasionally coming into the kitchen to show me where something was or how to cook a dish.

"Wow," Tana says, walking into the kitchen.

"Yeah, yeah, I know," I say, looking over the huge mess I made. "I said I could cook. I didn't say I was a neat cook."

Andi walks back out of the cooler after putting something away. "You were a rock star, as usual," she says to Tana. "Thank you."

"I'm just glad Mason was here to help out. It made the day a lot easier. Now, let's get this kitchen cleaned up."

"No way," Andi says, holding her hand up to Tana. "I'll get this. You go home to that sweet baby girl. It's already later than your usual time."

"Lucas has Iris, so I can stay if you need me."

"I'll stay and help her close up." The fact that I'm about to be in this place alone with Andi makes the hair on my arms stand.

"Yeah," Andi chimes in. "We've got this. Have a good night."

It isn't long before Andi and I are leaning against the wall, looking over the sparkling, cleaned and sanitized kitchen, waiting for the dishwasher to finish. She lets out an exhausted breath and wipes her brow with her forearm.

"Just a few more minutes, and then you'll be rid of me," I joke.

"I owe you."

"You don't owe me shit."

"Yeah, I do. If you didn't step up to help me today, I don't know what I would've done."

"Please. You would have powered through like the badass you are. I can see it's stressful, but you aren't the type to just lay down and die."

The corner of her lips tip up, and she angles her head toward me. "No. I'm not."

A smudge of chocolate from the éclair cake she made to put in the cooler for tomorrow's dessert sits on her jawline. I've never had a big sweet tooth, but I can't stop myself from imagining licking it off her skin.

"Why are you staring at me?" she asks, the smile still on her beautiful face.

"Looks like I'm not the only messy one in the kitchen."

My hand shakes as I swipe my fingers across her smooth skin, cleaning the chocolate away. Her smile fades as I sink deeper into her blue eyes.

Back away, Mason. You're just going to hurt her. Before I can make myself walk out of this diner before mistakes are made, she moves first, pressing her body against me. All sense of responsibility flees as she pulls my head down the few inches to meet her lips. If I don't stop this before it's too late, my world could come crashing down.

CHAPTER TWO

Andi

THE SOFT ORANGE glow from the ambient lighting in this tiny corner coffee shop is giving me all kinds of ideas on how to redecorate the diner. It's been a while since I've been to Birkenshire. Hell, it's been a while since I've been anywhere since I took over the diner. I struggle to find the time to clean my house, much less any amount of self-care. But thanks to Tana, my ashy-brown hair no longer looks like I dipped the bottom two inches into blonde hair dye. My nails are no longer jagged and have a beautiful shade of ballet pink that matches my newly manicured toes.

"I'm telling you," Tana says as she sips her pumpkin spice latte, "that dark chocolate hair color is amazing on you."

"I'm glad you talked me into it. I love it." I run my fingers through my soft curls that flow just past my shoulders. "I've been dying my hair blonde for so long, I couldn't even imagine my hair this color. Change is in the air, I guess. I just pray that the people in Cresna can handle the change at the diner." I cringe and slap my hand over my mouth. Tana made me promise her not to talk about the diner today when she picked me up this morning. I've failed at least seventeen times and got shushed each one.

Tana sighs with a grin and places her cup onto the white saucer. "They'll get used to it, and I think once they are, they're going to love it so much more than they already do. Besides, it's not like you're taking things off the menu or anything. Just changing up a few days."

The anxiety that Tana has been successfully keeping at bay by not letting me talk about the diner today has risen like a flash flood in the desert. One minute, my feet are on dry solid ground, and the next, I feel like I'm over my head in water. "I hope you're right. Or I'll be solely responsible for taking out the longest living business in Cresna."

"But we all agreed with you. I didn't even know if Brice had teeth in his mouth because I've never seen him smile until you came to us with this idea. Everyone is going to get more time with their families, so think about it that way."

Tana's right. This new change in hours is going to be an amazing adjustment for me. The diner has always been open seven days a week, morning to night. But finding new waitstaff in this little town is next to impossible, and since I'm now having to do all of the back-end business of owning a restaurant, the time I have to be actually waiting tables is slim. So, the diner will be open regular hours Tuesday through Thursday. Friday and Saturday we will have a limited menu other than pizza and won't be open until two in the afternoon. Sunday we'll only be open for breakfast, and Mondays are now closed. It's a huge change for this tiny community.

"I just hope this trial run with Jessica running the diner while we're gone works. Otherwise, my plan to have her running the place on Sundays is out, and I'm back to working six days a week."

"It's going to be great. Jessica is awesome, and I know she can handle it." She reaches across the table and gives my hand a comforting squeeze before grabbing her cup again and tilting the last drops into her mouth.

"Thank you for today." The sting of how much today meant to me hits the back of my eyes. It's been a long time since I've had a close friendship with anyone, and Tana has become the best friend I always told myself I didn't need. I was wrong.

"I'm just glad I didn't have to hog-tie you to get you in my car."

Tana's phone rings through our giggles from her purse. Her face lights up as she pulls it from her bag and sees the name on the screen. "I'm sorry, I have to answer this, or his mind will go to bad places," she says.

"Of course, girl. Take it."

"Hi, honey," she answers. The happiness and love fills her aura, and I grin enviously as I reach for my phone as if I have anything even remotely to look at that will bring me the same kind of joy. I pull up the decorating blog I follow to scroll while she talks, but before I get two scrolls in, Tana pushes in close next to me in the booth and sticks her phone out in front of us.

"Wow," Lucas gasps as his eyes widen on the screen in the video call. "You both look like you've had a great day. Hey," he calls, angling his eyes away from his screen. "Come check this out."

I nearly swallow my tongue as Lucas moves his phone and Mason comes into view. From the look on his sun-kissed face, he's just as shocked to be seeing me as I am him. His hazel eyes stare back at me, mouth hanging open for a second before he rubs his chin. "The color suits you," he stutters. "You look...um...I like..." He stops talking when Lucas smacks him on the shoulder.

"Jesus," Lucas whispers but not low enough for us not to hear. Tana giggles as Lucas rolls his eyes and walks away from Mason.

"Iris wants pizza and cartoons tonight. You good with that, or would you rather do something else?" he asks. Tana gets up from the booth and takes her seat across from me.

I can't hear any more of their conversation because my mind is filled with visions of the night at the diner when Mason pierced me with his hazel eyes and touched his full lips to mine two weeks ago. When I forgot all about the kind of woman I've become and let myself be free for once. Remembering how dizzying the feeling of his powerful hands on my body felt. Reliving the pain of his rejection when he pushed me away from him just as things got heated. The regret lives on inside of me for throwing myself at him and not being able to stomach seeing him ever since. Which made the fact that he stopped coming into the diner again a relief instead of a letdown.

"Andrea?" Tana calls, and I jump in my seat. "Good grief, are you okay?"

"I'm fine." I pick up my cup and sip the last little bit of my chai tea. "Just tired after a long day of unusual pampering. I'm ready whenever you are."

"Won't be unusual for long. We're going to make a point to do this more often. You can't keep going the way you were. Nobody can."

As Tana drives back to Pine Valley, I can't help but stare at the sun as it descends behind the mountains in the distance. The orange hue of the sky makes all the changing leaves look like glowing embers across the horizon. So many people love spring and say it's the sign of new life. But my heart belongs to the fall with winter right behind it. Both seasons come with the social acceptance of staying inside your house and being a little bit of a recluse. Every other time of the year, I'm just the oddball on the street that only comes outside to sit on her porch steps when there's a rare cool breeze. Truth is, I don't care anymore what people think about me. I used to. But that part of me is gone, and I can't say I miss her too much. Life became easier for me when I just stopped. Stopped trying. Stopped looking. Stopped loving.

We turn onto Tana's street, and my heart sinks. Mason's car is parked behind mine in front of Lucas and Tana's duplex. Thankfully, there's no one in front of me, blocking me in. But just knowing he's here makes me fidgety.

"You want to come in for a minute?" Tana asks, putting her car in park and turning off the engine.

"Nah, looks like you already have company."

"All right. I've tried to keep my nose out of it, but I'm done. What is going on between you and Mason?"

"Nothing. I don't know what you're talking about." I reach for the door handle, and Tana grabs my arm.

"I saw the look on your face when he popped into the video call earlier. Lucas says he makes all kinds of ridiculous excuses not to go to the diner for lunch with the guys from work. You two looked like you had been together for years at the wedding, and there was definitely some heat between you at the diner a few weeks ago. Now, it seems like the two of you can barely stand to look at each other. So spill it."

I squeeze my eyes shut and pinch the bridge of my nose. "Nothing. I mean...we get along fine...it's just..." I open my eyes, and Tana taps her fingers onto her crossed arms. "Things got a little hot and heavy the night of the wedding. But I stopped it. I pushed him away. So when he kind of disappeared after that, I figured maybe he was pissed about it. Maybe he thinks I led him on and stopped right before I put out."

"If he's pissed because you didn't want to have sex, I'll kill him," she says.

I grab her arm this time. "Before you kill him, just listen. The night he helped me at the diner, I threw myself at him. I kissed him, and just like before, it got heated fast between us, and I was all in this time. But then he pushed me away. He didn't talk the rest of that night while we finished closing up and haven't talked to each other since. Well, until today, I guess. I'm not sure what happened."

"Sounds like you both are throwing out some mixed signals. I think you two should talk and get this straightened out. He's Lucas's best friend, and you're mine. It's inevitable that you'll run into him again and probably often." Tana's daughter, Iris, runs out the front door of her duplex. "We'll talk later," she says. I nod, and we both get out of the car.

"Mommy! Uncle Mason came! He brought me a new horsey!"

"So cool," Tana says to Iris. "What's its name?"

"Mason!" Iris shouts, and Tana laughs, then turns to me. "You sure you don't want to come in?"

Lucas and Mason step outside, and my eyes connect with Mason's fiery stare. "I'm sure. I'll see you Tuesday?"

"You will. Bright and early."

I nod, scurry to my car, and get the heck out of Mason's line of view. Because those eyes are dangerous. They pull me in and make my body feel things that I haven't felt in years. Some good and some I'd rather not feel again. I made a decision a long time ago that I'm not going down this road again. For Lucas and Tana's sake, I need to make it clear to Mason that nothing will be happening between the two of us and we should try to get along.

Tana's right—it's impossible to avoid him. I've realized over the last few weeks just how damn small this town is. Especially since Mason only lives a few streets away from me. Every time I turn around, I see his car or work truck buzzing about. Even though I've gotten pretty damn good at dodging him, it's become tiresome. Better to get things cleared up, and who knows, maybe we can be friends. I just have to keep my hands and my lips to myself, and everything will be fine.

I'll be happy when Lucas and Tana finally move into their

new house in Cresna next week. It's not that I hate the drive from Pine Valley, but it isn't my favorite. Especially once the sun goes down and the animals come out. I can't wait until she's only a minute out of town instead of twenty. As I enter town, the muscles in my neck loosen. I glance at the diner as I pass and take the second right on Palmetto Avenue. One block down, I pull into the driveway of a house that used to belong to my grandparents and park.

I love this house, and they knew it. Which is why they left it to me. As I step out of my car, memories of skipping up the sidewalk when I was a young girl coming for Easter pop into my head, and I smile. As my foot hits the first step up to the porch, I raise my eyes, and that smile fades. The door is open. *Never walk into a house with an open door.* I can hear my daddy's words of caution in my head and as my heart races. I back away from the porch, run to my car, and jump in. My hands shake as I dial 911.

The dispatcher probably thinks I'm a complete moron as I stumble over my words and forget my own address for a second. I start the engine, back out of the driveway, and park on the street across from the house so I can see the front door in case someone comes out. There's no reason that door should be open. I always pull on the handle after I walk out to make sure I locked it, and I know for a fact I did that this morning when I left. No one has a key to this house except for my parents, and they don't even live in the same state. Something is very wrong here.

emanating around her. I've only seen her a little on edge once before when Tana was in trouble. It scared all of us. But this look in her eye is making me feel a certain way. Those cops better come back here and say what I want to hear. If someone is fucking with Andi, they aren't going to like what happens when Lucas and I figure out who they are.

I move to her and put my arm around her shoulder, and she rests her head on my chest. Her soft hair brushes against my jaw, and I breathe her in. Holding Andi in my arms feels just as good as it did the last two times. I've known her for much longer than a few months, but it was always in the diner or some event with Tana and Lucas. That wedding brought something out of us that had been building up for some time. *Stop thinking about it, you idiot.*

As we stand in the middle of the street waiting for the police to finish clearing the house, neither of us moves or talks. A few minutes pass, and Tucker comes out of Andi's house, followed by the two other officers. Andi lifts her head and removes her body from my hold, and I step forward with her as Tucker gets closer.

"The house is clear. Nothing looks suspicious, and there's no signs of a forced entry anywhere."

"That's impossible," Andi says, shaking her head.

"If you're sure you locked that door, I would double-check who has keys and see where they are right now. You said your parents have keys, right?"

"They do, but they live in Wisconsin, and I texted my Mama. They're home. No one else has keys."

Tucker twists his lips. "I'll keep an eye on the house, do some extra patrols. But other than that, there's nothing else I can do. I would suggest getting a security system and changing your locks just to be safe. You can call me anytime if anything else comes up," he says. "You've got my number." Everyone in town has Tucker's number. He was born and raised right here in Cresna.

"I will. Thank you."

Tucker and I exchange a nod before he goes back to his cruiser, and the three drive away.

"Fuck," Andi spits, then digs in her pocket and pulls out her car keys.

"Where are you going?" I ask as she turns her back to me.

"I'm moving my car out of the road and back into the driveway. Thanks for stopping." I really hate the waver in her voice.

"Whoa." I reach out, grasp her arm, and spin her to face me again. "You think I'm just going to leave you like this?"

"You heard them. Everything is fine. There's no evidence anyone was in my house. But I don't know how the hell I'm going to sleep tonight."

"The house might be fine, but from the water gathering in your eyes, you are not. Go park your car, I'll park mine, and I'll go in with you."

"You really don't have to do that," she says, glancing down at my thumb that decided on its own to caress the skin it landed on.

"If you think for one second that I'll be able to sleep knowing that you're over here freaking out, you're crazy."

"Okay. I kind of need to talk to you anyway."

My interest is piqued on what Andi needs to talk to me about. She parks her car far to the side of the driveway. I made the right decision to stay, seeing her stare at her front door while she holds herself again as I park. She jumps at the thud from my car door closing, and I rush to her side. I have always been one to let the lady lead, guiding her by the small of her back. But Andi stills when I try to guide her forward.

"You first," she says. The forced playful smile on her face hits me like a brick. I hate that she's afraid.

I take a few steps toward her small front porch, and my body wants to freeze when I feel her cold hand wrap around my arm and squeeze. I knew a long time ago that Andi was different. That I needed to stay away from her in order to keep the promise I made to myself. She could threaten everything I have overcome up to this point in my life. But the fact that I won't be able to live with myself if anything were to happen to her is the reason I'm staying.

We make our way up the porch, I open the door, and we step inside. Andi releases my arm and takes off her sandals. The light tapping of her bare footsteps trails across the living room through a large opening to the kitchen. Her eyes dart around, inspecting every inch.

"Everything look okay?"

"I think so. It's all just too weird and doesn't make any sense."

The inside of Andi's house is nothing I would have expected. Some older homes can feel dark and a bit dreary. But even at night, this place glows inside. The cream-colored walls balance the dark hardwood floors. A chunky white blanket lies in a mess on her light gray sofa in front of the picture window. The only thing that feels old in the room is the brick fireplace in the corner.

"Are you just going to stand at the door, or are you coming in?" Andi asks from the kitchen.

I kick off my shoes, walk past a long hallway to the left, and join her in the kitchen, which has a small dining room table to the right. This room feels even brighter than the living room. Mostly because of the bright white cabinets and crystal light fixtures. But a little because Andi is standing in it. She grabs an electric kettle from the white stone counter next to the sink and fills it with water.

"Want tea?"

"Depends what kind."

She places the kettle onto the electric base, presses a button, and reaches into the cabinet. She grabs a box and tosses it in my direction.

"Um, are you sure you want to drink this right now?"

"Yep." Her curt responses have nothing to do with me. She's tough, but this is not her normal self.

"This is black tea with extra caffeine."

"Do you want some or not?"

"No, thanks." I walk across the kitchen and place it on the counter next to her. "I'll be up for days if I drink that."

"That's the plan," she says, barely looking at me and moving around the horseshoe-shaped kitchen like she can't stand still to save her life, ping-ponging from one counter to another. She grabs milk from the fridge, walks back to the kettle, and places it on the counter. She moves across the kitchen again, grabbing a mug from another cabinet, and slams it shut. Halfway back to where I'm standing by the sink, she drops the mug, and it shatters on the floor.

"Fuck. Motherfucker. God dammit. Son of a bitch."

I push off the counter, but before I can, she's frantically picking up the pieces with her hands.

"Stop." I place my hand on her shoulder first, but it's like I'm not even there. "Andi, stop." I kneel down and catch her wrist gently, but she's still picking at pieces. "Stop! Andrea."

Her body stills, and her eyes blink up to mine. "I'm sorry." Tiny dimples start to appear on her chin as she fights her bottom lip from quivering.

"Don't apologize." I carefully pluck the pieces of broken pottery out of her hand as she stares at me. Relieved she didn't cut herself, I lay the pieces on the floor in a tiny pile. I pull her up from the ground, put my hands on her hips, and hoist her onto the counter.

"There's a little broom and dustpan under the sink," she says, pointing.

I clean up the broken mug, toss the pieces into the trash, and move back to her. "I know you're freaked-out. But the police checked everywhere. There's no sign that someone broke through that door. And even if there was…" The kettle beeps, and if I wasn't watching close enough, I would have missed her barely there jolt. "I'm here, and someone would have to go through me to get to you. So release that tension in your shoulders, and stop grinding your teeth. Everything is okay."

She nods, and electricity flows through my body when she grips my arms as she steadies herself and hops down from the counter.

"Thank you for picking that up." She tucks a piece of her dark brown hair behind her ear, gets a new mug, and walks a little slower back to the kettle. I take a breath, happy I was able to calm her down a bit. "I was visiting my parents in Wisconsin a few years ago when I was robbed at gunpoint. So what happened tonight doesn't feel so good."

My blood stills in my veins. No fucking wonder she's so afraid right now. "Did he hurt you?" I ask, clenching my teeth like I just told her not to.

"No." The weight on my chest lifts. She pours the hot water over the tea bag she placed in her new mug, and she cradles it in her hands. "Do you want anything? Snack? Beer?"

"Beer sounds great."

She grabs one from the fridge, hands it to me, and waves for me to follow her as she takes a loud sip of her tea.

"Isn't that too hot still?"

She laughs. "My mama says I probably singed all of my taste buds off a long time ago. I like it hot." She moves the blanket over her lap as she sits down, reaches behind her, and pulls the cord to close the blinds on the picture window. I sink into the softest couch I've ever sat on.

"Holy shit. This is a comfortable couch."

From the grin on her face, I'm not the only one in desperate need of a subject change. "It's the best, isn't it? I waited until I found the perfect one for this room. It took eight months to be delivered." Pride flows from her pores as her eyes dance around the room.

I open my beer and take a long drink. "I wasn't expecting it to look like this inside."

"This house is so special to me. I remember running down that hallway on Christmas morning and my grandma sweeping me up into her arms before I could reach the presents. My mama always dragging behind my daddy because she hated mornings so much," she says with a laugh. "We spent every holiday with my family all shoved into this small house. Even though I updated a few things and painted the walls, all of my best memories live on inside of them. My grandma knew how much I loved being here. That's why she left this house to me." She takes another sip of her tea, places the cup onto the coffee table in front of us, and sinks back into the corner of the couch, snuggling the cover up to her chin.

"You're lucky. I don't have anything like that. I'm a military brat. We never stayed in the same place for too long. I was used to it, but I never had a concrete foundation to attach myself to."

"That's sad."

I shrug. "For me, a house is just some sticks."

"I don't know what I would have done without this place. Fights with my mama, trouble with the girls at school… heartbreak." Pain covers her face, and I flinch. "This house is where I got through all of it. It's my safe place. And the fact that I didn't feel safe when I came home tonight is killing me."

"You're safe with me."

"I'm sure you learned all kinds of ways to kill someone in prison." Right after it comes out of her mouth, she regrets it. Her eyes grow large, and the remorse is thick in her heavy breath. "Oh fuck. I'm so sorry. I didn't mean it like… I was trying to be funny. Shit. Mason, I'm sorry."

"It was funny," I say, smiling. There's no way I'd let her know her words just gave me an internal paper cut. "And yeah, I did."

"Did you…" She hesitates and covers her mouth with the blanket.

"Did I what?"

"Are the rumors true? Did you go to prison because you killed someone?"

I can't help but bust out a laugh. "No. But I really, really wanted to."

Her eyes sparkle as two deep dimples set in on either side of her tipped-up lips, and she lays her head against the back of the couch. Her smile fades as she twists the thick yarn of her blanket with her long fingers.

"Were you pissed off at me that I backed away at the wedding?"

"Pissed?" I ask, shocked that she would think I was. "I would never be angry at a woman for not doing something she doesn't want to do."

"Then why did you stop coming into the diner?"

"Wasn't sure if you wanted me in there after that night." *God you're a fucking liar. It's not about her.* "Thought I'd give you some space."

"But then you saved my ass that night, and when I kissed you, you pushed me away."

I take a deep breath, set my beer bottle on the coffee table, and twist toward her. "I'm kind of a terrible person."

One side of her lips tip up. "You said I was safe with you."

"I can protect you from just about anything. Just not me. I'm terrible at relationships, and by terrible, I mean I don't do relationships."

She snort laughs and smacks her forehead. "Neither do I.

That's why I stopped you at the wedding. With the diner, I don't think I could handle a relationship right now."

We both chuckle, and her shoulders lose a little more tension. "We should have had this conversation a long time ago," she says. "We both agree that we should just be friends."

I nod. "Yep. That's it, and for the record, I'm a fucking stellar friend."

"It would appear."

I am a damn good friend, but I'm a lying fool if I think for one second I'm going to be able to only look at her as a friend. She yawns, and I spot her still-full cup of tea.

"You should get some rest."

"Will you stay?"

"If you would have asked me to leave, I would have camped outside of your house in my car." I'll torture myself to save her from me. But I like Andi, and the way she's sinking those aquamarine eyes into me right now only proves how fucking hard this is going to be. "I'm glad you're letting me stay in here though. This couch is going to be so much better than the leather car seats."

"Thank you." The tone in her soft voice soothes me. She gets up from the couch, takes her cup into the kitchen, and stops just before the hallway. "Do you want me to shut the lights off?"

"I'll get them in a few minutes after I make sure everything is all locked up."

"Good night, Mason."

"Good night."

The click of her bedroom door echoes down the hallway, and I get up, throw away my beer bottle, and check that every window and door in the kitchen and living room are locked. I turn the lights off and lie down on the couch, covering myself with the blanket Andi just had over her body. That was a mistake. It smells like her. A little bit of sweet mixed with the perfect touch of musk. I turn on my side, set my phone alarm for five, and close my eyes.

BOOM! I jump off the couch, still half-unconscious, when I hear Andi screaming. I run down the hallway as the door at the end slams open and she runs right into me. She screams again as her fists begin flying in my direction.

"Get the fuck out of my house!" she screams.

"Andi, it's me." I dodge a punch to the face, and she hits me in the shoulder. "It's Mason. It's okay."

Another crack of thunder shakes the house, and she jumps into my arms. "Shit. I forgot you were here. I'm sorry."

"Geez, you've got an arm on you."

"Something hit my window."

Still holding on to her, I take long, fast steps to the living room. "Stay here," I tell her, ripping open the front door and running outside. The pouring rain soaks me before I get down the front steps. The sky lights up, revealing a large tree branch that fell against the house just outside of Andi's window. A clap of thunder makes me run a little faster back into the house.

"Did you see anything?"

I shut the door behind me. "You heard a big tree limb fall, but everything else is fine."

"Thank God." Her chin falls to her chest as she places her hand over her heart. "I'm pretty sure my heart is in good shape, or I'd have already had a heart attack today." She lifts her head, and her mouth drops. "Good grief. You're soaking wet."

"I'm fine."

"You are not. Come on," she says. "I've got something for you."

I follow her down the hallway, making a point to keep my eyes from her legs adorned with silk-and-lace shorts. "I don't care how miserable I am, I'm not putting on your clothes. You'd probably take pictures and send them to Lucas."

She laughs, but my smile fades the moment I step foot into Andrea Taylor's bedroom. It doesn't match the brightness of the rest of the house. Its dark gray walls are dimly lit with two lamps on either side of a black upholstered bed. The only brightness the room gets is from the fluffy white linens and the peppering of rainbows from her crystal sconces on the wall.

"You okay?" she asks as she comes out from what I assume is a closet and catches me staring at her bed.

"How many fucking pillows does one person need?"

"That answer is seven, and if you say anything bad about my pillows, the friendship that we just solidified will be null and void."

Amused, I put my hands up. "No judgment here." Truth is, that bed looks like a fucking cloud. "You don't mess around with cozy, do you?"

"Not a chance. Here." She hands me a shirt and a pair of shorts.

"Please tell me these are not some ex-boyfriend's left-behinds."

"You're in luck. They aren't. They're my dad's. He left them here the last time they visited, and I told him I wasn't giving them back because I sleep in the shirt sometimes."

"Thanks. Are you okay now?"

"Yes. I'm used to storms, but tonight…"

"You have to stop trying to justify yourself. I get it."

"You're right," she says. "You are a good friend."

"Damn right," I say, flashing her a wink and walking out of her bedroom. I head into the living room, peel my wet shirt from my body, and kick off my jeans.

"Whoa my God! Umm…shit…sorry." I spin around, and Andi has her hands over her eyes.

"Wanted to get a peek, huh?" I tease, and she drops her hands.

"Absolutely not. Most people would change in a bathroom when they're at someone else's house."

"I assumed you were going back to bed."

Andi's eyes skimming over my chest and down to my boxer briefs as she bites her bottom lip is doing nothing for my willpower to stay away from her. It's not lost on me that she's just as attracted to me as I am to her. The rain hits harder against the windows as my phone chimes from the coffee table with an alert.

"I could have told them there's a severe thunderstorm five minutes ago," I say, pulling up the radar. "Wow, that's a lot of red."

"Let me see." Andi hurries to my side just as another crack of thunder booms around us. Her body jumps, and she grabs onto me. I instinctively wrap my arm around her, and she slowly lifts her head, her nervous breath tickling my skin. She should back up. I should let go. Instead, she pushes up on her toes as I lean my head down to get closer to her. Her eyes search mine, like she's waiting for me to give her a reason to walk out of this room. I could give her a thousand reasons why, but as her fingertips grip me tighter, I can't speak. Instead, I drop my phone to the ground and crash my lips onto hers.

She breathes in deeply through her nose as her hands wildly move across my back. With one arm around her waist, I lift her feet from the floor. The pressure from her legs wrapping tightly around my hips drives me crazy. I fill my hand with her soft, messy hair as her hard, deep kiss matches mine, and my lips burn with desire like never before. I walk until Andi's back is up against the hallway wall. A small groan comes from her throat as I move my lips to her jaw and grip her ass.

"Take me to bed," she moans.

"I thought we were just friends?" I ask between kisses.

"We are," she says, tugging my hair just enough to raise my eyes to hers. "Just friends," she pants.

"You're right. We shouldn't be doing this."

I can hardly breathe as I set her on her feet and take a step back. The lightning flashes, and the heat in the air between us could combust. The rumble of the sky shakes the house the same way Andi shakes me when she looks at me. The fire hasn't burned out of her eyes as they sink into mine. She bites her lip, and the friction between us grows.

At the same time, we lunge for each other, pushing that heat into our bodies. I take her mouth as if it were mine. Wishing it was mine. It isn't and never will be. Just as that thought pours cold water over the flame inside of me, she puts her hand on my ass and pulls me hard against her, fanning the fire again. Our tongues dance in the blaze as our hands travel the other's body.

The storm rages outside as I lift her again and carry her down the hall into her bedroom. I set her back on her feet in front of the bed. Heat hits my skin as she takes in every inch of me and wets her bottom lip. The desire radiates in her beautiful blue eyes, and I take a few steps back, remembering who the hell I am. My chest heaves from the fevered and desperate kiss, and it only gets harder to breathe as she pulls her silk camisole over her head.

She saunters back to me, stopping just as her peaked nipples graze my chest. The lightning outside has nothing on the electricity coursing through my veins. She is easily the most perfect woman I've ever seen. I want her more than I've ever wanted anyone else. A shiver rolls through me as she trails her hand from my rib cage down to my boxer briefs.

"Andi," I whisper in her ear and feel her sharp inhale. "I'm no good for you."

It's the worst possible time to repeat this, but I have to say it. She has to know what she won't be getting out of this. I'm giving her the out if she wants it. Her hands pause their descent down into the band of my boxers, and my heart falls. She gets up on her tiptoes, pressing her cheek against mine, her breath heavy on my ear.

"I know," she whispers back, then takes me in her hand and starts running her fingers over my tip.

Fuck. Is she seducing me? That's new. My head falls back as she strokes me, vulnerable in her soft, delicate hand. I'm getting those electric jolts in my fingertips and toes too soon. She's too beautiful, too smart, too fucking perfect. The smack of my hands on the ass of her silk pajama shorts echoes in the room as I pick her up and toss her onto the bed.

She gasps and grins as her tits bounce when she lands on the soft white fabric.

"Stay here," I say, and she nods. I jog to the living room, grab a condom from my wallet, and run back to her, tossing it onto the nightstand next to us. I tug her shorts and underwear down her legs and toss them behind me. Her body glows in the low lighting, and if I wasn't so damn aware of how much I'm torturing myself right now, I'd think this was a dream. With each kiss from her ankle to the inside of her thigh, I hate myself a little bit more.

She groans as I twist her nipple between my fingers and take my first taste of her, realizing that I will never be the same after this. With every glide of my tongue, her body shifts, and the light illuminates all her perfect curves and valleys. Her chest heaves with every flick of my tongue over her core as she grips my hair, and her thighs start to tighten. Her hips buck against my mouth as she comes undone, and I get drunk on her. As her moans slow, she pulls my face until it's even with hers. I place a hard kiss on her lips, grab the condom, and put it on. My erection rubs against her wet center, and I slowly bury myself inside of her on a growl.

The wind picks up outside as I create my very own storm in my chest. I was right. From the first day I met Andrea Taylor, I knew she wasn't like anyone I've ever met. She was something I could never have. I came to terms with that a long time ago. I had no idea this moment would happen or that it would affect me as much as it is right now.

As I rock our bodies together and get a small glimpse of what heaven is like, I watch her come undone for a second time. Her fingernails dig into my arms as I thrust harder, sending her further into climax and coming into my own. With rain and hail pelting the windows, I let the high of my release flow through my body as she stares straight into my soul. I slow my pace until the only movement between us is our heaving chests.

Andi smiles like she's just broken into a candy shop. This woman is something else. I shake my head in amusement and kiss her, hard, deep, and long. If we know what's good for both of us, this will be the last time I'll ever touch her lips, and I fucking hate it.

I pull back, brush a piece of her hair out of her face, and push myself away from her.

"I'll be right back," I say, not wanting her to think I'm leaving. I go into the bathroom, clean myself up, put on my pants, and criticize myself in the mirror for a minute before going back to Andi. Two steps into the bedroom door and I stop. "Um, Andi?"

"Yeah?" she says, still lying on the bed with twitching thighs.

"I'm pretty sure that whole goddamn tree is down." I point, and she jumps up to look. We jog to the window, and the huge oak tree that stood in the front yard of Andi's house is on the ground. The tree limbs barely missed both of our vehicles and landed in the street.

"Holy shit! Did you look around? There's more than just my tree down."

Instant dread hits me. "Fuck."

"What?"

"I'm a roofer, Andi. My feet aren't going to be on the ground anytime soon with all this damage. I hope nobody got hurt. Check your phone. I'll check mine."

"Oh my God," she says. "I hope the diner's okay. Oh God, I'm in charge of that now. Shit. What am I going to do if…"

"There is no use in freaking out at this moment, and if there's something that needs fixing at the diner, we'll get it fixed. Lucas and I know a hell of a lot of people. But I wouldn't worry about that yet. There aren't a lot of trees around the diner. I'm sure it's fine."

"Wow. You're good at that."

"I'm good at a lot of things, babe. Be more specific." I grin at her shaking head.

"You are unbelievable, Mason King. I meant, being logical and talking me down in record time. I'd be freaking the hell out right now."

She grabs a robe from behind her closet door and follows me out into the living room. I have about ten text messages from Lucas letting me know that they're okay and wondering if I'm good. Andi grabs her phone and jumps up to sit on the kitchen counter just in my line of view from the couch. I text Lucas back, then check the town's social media page. There's a post from the village warning the residents to stay in their houses until the storm has fully passed and the village crew can clean up the roads.

"Looks like a lot of the roads are blocked," I say, walking into the kitchen and holding my phone up for her to read the post too. "I could walk home."

"Absolutely not. What if you step on a power line or something? Most injuries occur after the storm is gone, you know."

She yawns and leans her head against the cabinets behind her. This is the moment I was dreading. The one where I want to take her back to bed, curl up behind her, and hold her until the morning. The moment when I know I shouldn't do that. Her eyes suddenly widen, her body stiffens, and she sits up on the counter, terror on her face.

"Andrea? What is it?"

"I…that's not…"

The hair on my arms and the back of my neck stands on end. "What the fuck is happening, Andi?"

She raises her arm, and her trembling finger points to the counter by the back door. Water pools in her eyes, and she jumps off the counter and runs out of the house. I try to stop her, afraid she might get hurt in the mess from the storm, but she catches me off guard. I follow her through the front door to her car. She rips open the driver's-side door and digs in the center console.

"Andi, tell me what the hell is going on." I'm confused but ready to pull whatever trigger I need to, to get the fear off her face.

She straightens from the car, the gentle rain dripping down her face as she holds up two keys. Her voice shakes as she speaks. "My main house key is on my car key ring." She holds up the key she just dug out. "This is my spare key. That key on the counter is not my key."

CHAPTER FOUR

Andi

CHAINSAWS AREN'T USUALLY part of my morning wake-up routine, but here we are. I stretch, moaning as my legs reach that cool part of the sheets, and pull my comforter up to my chin. The house is quiet, even though I know Mason is still here. After I found that key on my counter, he looked like murder was on his mind. Mine was inundated with how the hell someone got a key to my house and just let themselves in. If Mason wouldn't have been here with me, I'm not sure how I would have survived last night. But he kept assuring me that I'm safe and swore he'd stay awake and alert to make sure of it. I believe him.

Still, I can't wrap my head around who or why. I'm the most boring person in the world. I live, eat, sleep, and drink the diner. Not like I did much else before I bought it from the Mertzes. There's nothing missing, and everything looks to be just as I left it. Maybe Mama made another key and hid it outside? She used to do that at our old house. Especially since Daddy could never keep track of anything. But who used it to come inside, and why would they leave it on the counter?

As I lie in this bed, I keep coming up with more questions. It feels weird as hell to not already be at the diner by this time in the morning, but today starts the first day of our new weekend hours. Being off work yesterday with Tana was even more bizarre. I'll be anxious to hear all the details on how Jessica handled the place. It was only a week ago that I gave Jessica a key to the diner. Tana has a child, and if, God forbid, I get sick or something happens to me, I still need to make sure the diner is taken care of. Tana can only do so much, so I'm hopeful the rest of the crew will give me good feedback about how their day went.

I'm pulled from my thoughts as the front door opens and closes. Jumping out of bed, I speed walk to my closet, change into the first T-shirt and leggings I touch, and head out of my bedroom. The house is quiet, and my heart starts to beat faster.

"Mason?"

When I get no answer back, I move to the window in the front door and see Mason on the porch with Tucker, who's holding a chainsaw. The vein in this neck protrudes as he holds up the key and then points a finger in Tucker's face.

"You better fucking figure it out, Tuck." Mason's voice makes me pause as I open the door. Both of the men turn their heads to me.

"You're yelling at a cop, Mason," I remind him.

"No I'm not. He's not on duty. This is just the dumbass Tucker that lives next door to me and still owes me a six-pack after he drank mine."

"Oh Jesus," Tucker says, rolling his eyes. "Not this again."

"Hey," I interrupt. "Did you go past the diner? Does it look all right?"

"From what I could see, the front looked good. Didn't see the back though. There's a lot of branches down."

Damn. The back is what I'm worried about. That's the only side that has trees close enough to it.

"You're going to be here for a while, right?" Mason asks Tucker. The buzzing from chainsaws bounces off the houses from the village crews working on getting the streets clear of debris.

"Yeah, I'll be here a while."

"Good." Mason turns to me, moving his eyes down and back up my body. "I'll be right back."

"How long do you think you'll be? I was planning on heading to the diner soon to start prepping."

"Babe, there's no power. It went out a few hours ago just after you went to bed. Power company is estimating about six hours before they get it back on."

Tucker's head spins toward us. *Shit.* There's already going to be a smorgasbord of gossip going around town about why the cops were at my house last night. Now, we've just fed them sex and relationship dessert.

"After last night, you wouldn't have left any woman alone either. So don't even try."

Mason's cover brings me a little relief, but it's accompanied by a small pit in my stomach.

"Damn. I've got to make some phone calls before Jessica, Brice, and Tana try showing up to work."

"You do that. I'll be back." Mason pulls his keys from his pocket, nods at Tucker, and gives me the sexiest, fuck-you-later wink I've ever seen. I can't take my eyes from his ass as he walks to his car.

"I'll, uh…just be over here if you need me," Tucker says, the biggest grin spread on his face. He may have bought Mason's excuse for staying the night, but he didn't miss that wink or my reaction.

"We're just friends, Tucker. That's it."

"Yep. And I'm just the mailman." He chuckles as he walks back to the street to work on the tree.

After calling everyone off for the day, posting to our social media page that we'll be closed due to the storm, and talking to Tana, I toss my hair up into a bun and call Mama.

"Hey, sweetheart," she answers in her usual cheerful voice.

"Hey, Mama. We had a pretty nasty storm roll through here last night."

"Oh, I know."

She knows? "Are you and Daddy in town?" I ask, hoping to God they were and this is all just an insane mistake.

"I wish. We're in the camper by Chucktaw, and your father won't stop trying to get me to fish with him. I am *not* putting worms onto a hook and drowning them, only for them to get eaten. All just so he can take a picture with said fish and then toss the poor thing back into the lake with a new piercing it didn't ask for." She sighs. "How's the house? Everything okay?"

"Damn. It wasn't you," I say, talking to myself and then remembering Mama is on the phone. "Dramatic as always, Mama. The house is fine. There's a lot of damage in town though."

"What do you mean by it wasn't me?"

My insides twist as I would rather not tell Mama anything about the key. But it would be stupid of me not to let them know what's going on.

"I came home last night, and my front door was wide open."

"What? Tell me you didn't walk into that house by yourself, Andrea. Everyone always feels so safe in a tiny country town, but that's where some of the worst things happen."

"Gee, thanks, Mama."

"I'm sorry, honey. You just can't get too complacent and leave your doors unlocked."

"That's the thing. I don't leave my doors unlocked. Ever. Mason showed up when the cops were here and…"

"Stop right there," she says, her tone different than before. "The police? And who the hell is Mason?"

"I told you my door was open. I wasn't walking inside by myself. So I called the cops to go through the house. I've known Mason for a while now. He lives a few streets over, and he's also the best friend of Tana's husband."

"At least someone was there with you. What did they find?"

"Nothing. No marks on the door, and the windows were all still closed and locked."

"Maybe you didn't latch the door? We should come down. Your daddy can check things out."

"No." I shouted my resistance on accident. "You don't have to do that. I'm sure it was just not latched all the way." The more I'm talking to Mama, the more I don't want to tell her about the key. I love my parents, but they still feel like this is my grandma's house. Every time Mama comes, she ends up trying to redecorate and reorganize my home. It's exactly the way I want it, and for someone who doesn't drink very often, the wine seems to go down real nice when they come to visit. I do love having them close, just not under the same roof.

I gasp as my front door opens, and Mason walks in with a few plastic bags and what looks like a drill. "Sorry. Didn't mean to scare you," he says as I cover the speaker on my cell. The bags he brought in from the hardware store crinkle as he pulls out two brand-new door handles.

"Don't worry. Everything is fine here other than some tree branches down. I'll let you know if I need you."

"As long as you're sure. If you need us, just call and we'll be on our way. Trust me, I'd leave this damn campground in a heartbeat," she laughs. "I love you, Andrea."

"I love you too."

Mason tilts his head and flashes a quick glance at me as I end the call, and then the buzz of the drill sounds as he removes the old doorknob.

"This is kind of weird, don't you think?"

"What's weird now?"

"The fact that we've barely spoken since the wedding, and now overnight, you've become my knight in shining armor."

"I'll always care about your safety."

"I appreciate that. How much was it?" He shrugs and puts the new gorgeous black hardware on my front door. "That isn't how this is going to work. I ask you how much they cost, you tell me, and I write you a check."

"Don't worry about it."

"Mason…I…"

"This is what friends do," he snaps.

I decided a long time ago that relationships aren't worth the hassle, and I haven't missed being in one. But the way he just said that hits a nerve in my chest. "Is it?"

"Jesus. What kind of friends do you have? Yes. It is. We take care of each other. After I put this on, I'll know you are safer than you were with the old one. I think you need to get some cameras put up too."

"Yeah, probably." Add it to the ever-growing list of things I need to do.

"I went to the diner and checked the roof. There's a few spots that have wind damage and need repair. Lucas is going to meet me over there, and we'll get the areas tarped until we can fix them."

"You did all that in the time you were gone?"

"Gotta be quick. There's a lot of work in this town to get done. Mr. Murphy at the store said they're thinking there was a weak tornado that went through here."

"No way," I say, crossing my arms.

"If you saw town, you'd believe it."

"Are you telling me that we had sex in the middle of a tornado and didn't even know it?"

He stops the drill and slowly turns to me with a grin that could melt my panties right off my body. "I guess I'm just that good."

"I think I'm the one who deserves the accolades. You were putty in my hands."

He rises from his kneeled position in front of my open door, and my lungs beg for more oxygen with each of his steps toward me. I tilt my head back to look up into his eyes as he presses his body against mine and wraps his arm around my lower back. "Should I show you…"

"Hello?" A familiar voice comes from the front door. Mason and I both take a huge step back, separating our bodies, but it's too late. "What's going on in here?" Lucas says, sounding like he already knows the answer.

"I thought we were meeting at the diner," Mason says, walking back to the door.

"We were, but thankfully I didn't find any damage at the house, so I went to the diner, and you weren't there yet, so I assumed you were still here." He slaps Mason on the shoulder and walks across the living room to me. "Mason told me your door was wide open when you came home last night. If at any time you have any trouble and can't get a hold of Mason or Tucker, you call me. I'll be here. I don't care if it's three in the morning."

"Thank you for that."

"I don't know what the fuck has gotten into people lately," he says, pulling a cotton candy sucker from his pocket, ripping off the paper, and sticking it in his mouth. "They either have no idea who they're fucking with, or they have a death wish. One thing I know is we aren't about to let people mess around with our wives or girlfriends."

"We aren't..." I say.

"She's not my..." Mason stutters.

"We're just friends," I say as the sweat starts beading on my forehead.

"Yep. Nothing going on between us."

"Nope."

Lucas bounces his amused grin between Mason and me as we interrupt each other, trying to make our point. He chuckles and crunches down on the sucker. "Well, you two looked pretty damn friendly when I walked in just now."

"Whack," Mason warns, and Lucas throws his hands up. I've only heard Lucas called by his nickname a few times before. I'm not sure what it means, but Tana mentioned it's from when Lucas was in prison. In prison *with* Mason. I still can't get my mind around that, but as I've grown to know the men of Lucas's circle, they did bad shit but for good reasons. I don't know what Mason did to land him in prison, and nobody else seems to either. But as small towns go, there are so many rumors it's comical.

Lucas pulls his ringing phone from his pocket. "Here we go. The start of a long-ass day." He snarls as he presses on the screen, puts it up to his ear, and walks across the living room toward the door. "Redman's Roofing," he answers.

The moment Lucas walks outside, Mason stands, admiring his work for a moment, then grabs his drill and the other door handle. My lips begin to dry as he brushes against me on his way through the kitchen to the back door.

"If we're going to be just friends, I'm gonna need you to stop looking at me like that," Mason says, kneeling down and using his drill to remove the old doorknob.

I scrunch my face up. "How am I looking at you?"

"Like you want me to push you up against that wall and repeat last night."

"First of all, I'm not looking at you like that. And secondly, if we're going to be just friends, I'm going to need you to stop talking to me like that. Last night shouldn't have happened."

His head twists so fast in my direction, I think he could have broken his neck. "You regret it?"

I picture every mouthwatering, body-trembling moment of last night. "Not one bit." The deep wrinkles that appeared between his eyebrows disappear, and he goes back to working on the door. "I'm single. You're single. We're both adults."

His bright white smile spreads across his face, and Lucas walks back in. "Whenever you're done, we've got a list a mile long already. The roads in town are a disaster. You should just ride in my work truck."

"I'll be done in two minutes, and then you'll just have to follow me to drop off my truck at my house," Mason says.

"You can just leave it here. I mean, I know it's like a two-second drive, but I think I might feel a little better having another vehicle in my driveway."

"Tana is at home by herself since her mom has Iris for the day, and we have power in Pine Valley. You should go over there so you can eat and shower if you want."

"That sounds way better than staring at the walls of this house for the next six hours if that's how long it takes for the power to come back on. I'll call her."

An hour after Mason left with Lucas to go be heroes in the town, I sit down at Tana's table as she sets a cup of tea in front of me.

"I don't understand. How did someone get a copy of your house key?" she asks.

"It seems almost impossible. I'm trying to think if my grandma had a copy way back in my junk drawer, and when I pulled everything out the other day, maybe I missed it. To be honest, trying to figure it out is giving me a raging headache. I hope this tea has caffeine in it."

"It does," Tana says, taking a careful sip.

"Thank God. I was up all night." I close my eyes, knowing what I just said. Tana knows damn well Mason was at my house all night.

"Oh? All night, you say?" Her eyebrows bounce as she wiggles with glee in her chair.

"Montana Redman, don't do it."

"So did you two like, play cards? Perhaps a puzzle?"

Holding back my laugh is actually painful, but one thing I can't control is the heat I feel in my cheeks. I can only imagine the lovely shade of scarlet they're turning.

"It's about damn time you two stopped denying what you have. Everyone knows you two belong together. Thank God you've finally seen it too."

"Uh, not exactly. We aren't together."

"I'm sorry, what?"

"We're just friends. We both agreed that neither of us want anything to do with a relationship right now."

"Are you telling me he stayed with you all night, and you two kept your hands…and other body parts…to yourselves?"

"That's not exactly what I said." Tana's laugh echoes throughout her kitchen. "So my friend comes with a perk," I say, shrugging and matching her laugh. "Just do me a favor and let's keep this between us."

"Girl, your secret is always safe with me. But I really hope you two can find a little happiness with each other. However that happiness may come about doesn't matter."

"Anyway," I say, desperate to change the subject, "looks like you're almost all packed up." The boxes in Tana's duplex are stacked three and four high and are scattered throughout her living room and kitchen. "I wish I could help you tomorrow."

"Are you kidding me? You're going to be the hero tomorrow evening when you bring all those pizzas. All these guys are going to be hungry. This storm couldn't have come at a worse time though. With so many people in town needing help, I think Lucas and his crew are going to have a hard time getting to everyone today so we can start moving tomorrow. Thank God for the boys coming."

"It will be nice to see Everest and Owen again. How's Natalie doing?"

Tana and Lucas's wedding gave me a chance to get to know Lucas's circle of friends, and they are the most welcoming people I've ever met. Natalie and Owen were such sweet hosts and invited me to come back to their gorgeous lodge anytime. I was treated like an old friend, and it's no secret that I don't have a lot of those.

"The baby is keeping her up all night. I wish she lived closer so I could help her with Starling. I remember those nights well."

"Starling? What a gorgeous name."

"They have this thing with birds, and when they told us the name, we all fell in love. It's so perfect for her. We're planning to go to the lodge in a few weeks. I think Mason was planning on coming too. He's got his camper down there. You should come."

"I don't think I want to leave the diner for an entire weekend like that. Not to mention that seems a little…relationshippy to me," I say, shaking my head.

"Well, Jessica is in charge on Sundays now, remember. It would only be one day. And it's not *relationshippy*, but I get it. If you change your mind, you're more than welcome to come with us."

"Thanks. I'm glad Mason and I are friends, but I think the less time we spend together, the longer that will last."

———

I GLANCE at the clock on the wall next to the TV. The sun set well over an hour ago, and I thought Mason would have already picked up his work truck by now. I stayed at Tana's until Jessica texted me that the power was restored in Cresna. I figured Mason would be hungry by the time he was done with work, so I made a lasagna and packaged half of it up for him with a salad and garlic bread. But the later it gets, the more I'm convinced he just went home and left his truck here for the night.

My cozy blanket falls to the ground as I rise from the couch and head to my bedroom to change into my black satin pajama set. I have the same set in every single color they sold. Spending money on fashionable clothes, makeup, handbags, or shoes has never been my thing. Except for these pajamas. As the camisole floats down over my head and over my body, peace and calm come over me. When my pajamas go on at night, it's proof that I made it through today and tomorrow is a new start.

I walk into the kitchen, get myself a bowl of ice cream, and turn all the lights off on my way to the couch. I'm still anxious about the front door being open and the mysterious key we found, but I can't let this rule my life. So I ignore the strange feeling in the pit of my stomach every time I walk into a room and remind myself that Mason is only a phone call away. Before I cozy back up with my blanket, I light the candles I have placed on the coffee table, fireplace, and on either side of the TV. I grab my cell phone just in case, get back on the couch, and snuggle up with my bowl of mint chocolate chip. I put on the feel good romance movie I recorded last week and prepare myself for a good cry. There's nothing like watching two people fall in love. Maybe I'm broken because I don't feel like I'm missing out on love. Love is messy and painful and tends to change who I am inside. It took me a long time to repair all the damage inside of me from so-called *love*, and I'm not willing to let anyone take a machete to my soul again.

Halfway through the movie, a roar of an engine comes to a halt just outside of the house. I spin around, peek through the blinds, and see Mason stepping out of Lucas's truck with a tool belt in his hand. He waves Lucas off and walks to his identical company work truck parked in my driveway. A small twitch of disappointment hits my chest that he isn't going to come in as I settle back into the couch. *Jesus, Andrea. Why are you doing this to yourself? It's better that he goes home.*

A soft knock from the front door makes me jump. I get up, take a few steps, and open the front door. One look at Mason and I wish I hadn't because he looks extra hot. Exhausted but gorgeous. He leans into the arm that's stretched over his head and resting on the doorjamb. The sleeves have been torn off his company logo T-shirt and reveal his tan, muscled arms. His face, though, looks wrecked.

"Just wanted to make sure you're good. Need anything?" he asks.

"Oh my God. Are you okay?"

"Sore as hell, and exhausted, but I'll live."

"You look it. Wow."

Grabbing his chest, he pushes his eyebrows together, making deep wrinkle lines on his forehead. "Damn, woman. That hurt."

I laugh. "I made you some food. Step in here while I grab it so you don't let in the bugs."

He steps inside and closes and locks the door behind him as I walk to the kitchen, grab the containers from the fridge, and walk back to him.

He looks around the room, and then his eyes move down my body. "What is all this?" he asks, taking the containers from my hands.

"Lasagna, salad, and garlic bread."

His eyes close as he has a food orgasm right in front of me. "I'm so fucking hungry. You have no idea. I've had a banana all day. A banana. You didn't have to do this, but thank you." His body leans against the door as he stares over my shoulder. I've never seen him look so worn-out.

"Mason?"

"Yeah."

"Do you want me to heat this up for you? I'm just watching a movie. If you'd rather just go, that's up to you. But I really don't mind making you a hot plate while you chill on the couch."

"I'm not in the position to decline that offer. That sounds awesome."

I take the containers back from him. "Kick off your shoes and have a seat. Won't take long." The poor guy grunts as he bends down to untie his work boots and grunts on his way back up. No doubt he worked his ass off today.

After heating up the lasagna, I plate his food up and bring it to him in the living room. He's barely holding himself or his eyelids up. He takes the plate from me and adjusts himself on the couch. A few minutes later, his plate is empty.

"That was amazing. So good. Thank you."

I shrug. "It's what I do. I feed people." I take his plate, bring it to the kitchen, and rinse it off. As I walk back into the living room and sit back down, I notice he's leaning deep into the corner, holding his head up with his hand while his eyelids flutter.

"I should go home," he says, aiming his eyes at me. "You look so fucking pretty in this light," he mumbles as his eyelids close.

It's impossible not to take this moment to admire Mason's peaceful features. His full lips are slightly parted, just asking to be kissed. The sharp line of his jaw is softer as he sleeps. I just never noticed how tense it usually is. His rough hand rests over his chest as it rises and falls. I'm sure I should wake him up and tell him to go home, but I just don't have the heart to do it. I cover him up with the blanket, shut off the TV, blow out the candles, and head to bed.

Staring at the ceiling in my room, something doesn't sit right inside of me. Making him dinner. Wanting him around. In my house. *In my bed.* The same question keeps repeating over and over in my head, and I keep coming up with the same answer. *Can I be just friends with Mason?* No.

CHAPTER FIVE

MASON

THE PAST FEW days have been a bitch on my body. Every muscle is screaming, but there's still a lot of things to move from Tana and her mama's duplexes to their new property just outside of Cresna. We got most of the houses in town tarped yesterday by working into the night with spotlights until we just physically couldn't do it anymore.

I put a box labeled *IRIS* into her new room and head back out to grab another but find Lucas on the porch bench, taking a break. It's the first chance we've had two seconds to talk all day, so I take a seat next to him.

"I thought you might ditch out on me today," Lucas teases. He knows damn well I would never do that to him.

"And risk missing all of this fun? Never."

"There's still a bunch of donuts in the kitchen. I thought between you and I they'd be gone by now."

"I'm not that hungry. After I switched vehicles, I ran to the gas station and got a breakfast burrito."

"Sick. I can't believe you trust that gas station bacon." He tilts his head back and chugs an energy drink, but his eyes shoot to me mid gulp.

"What the fuck are you looking at me like that for?"

"You switched vehicles, huh?" *Shit.* "Does that mean you didn't go home last night?"

I shake my head. "It's not what you think. I passed out on her couch, got up this morning, and left. No big deal."

Leaving out a few details will only help my case. I can't tell him that I was mesmerized by the way the candlelight lit up the curves of her cheeks. Or how I couldn't take my eyes off her this morning when I went to the bathroom and saw her sleeping through the open bedroom door. How I wanted so badly to go to her, nuzzle her neck, and grip that sweet little ass that was sticking out of those silk shorts she has that drive me crazy. How I can't stop thinking about her.

"That's two nights in a row. I think you should stop being a dipshit and admit you like her." Lucas pulls his usual cotton candy sucker from his pocket and shoves it inside his cheek.

"We're just friends. Neither of us want a relationship."

"Uh-huh."

"I can't tell you how fucking happy I am for you and Tana. No one deserves to be happy in this world more than you. But you have to remember, not everyone wants the life you have."

"I don't get it, but all right. I'll stop pushing."

"Thank you." Relief comes over my body as Lucas ends the conversation about Andi and me when Everest and Owen find us.

"What the fuck is this? We work while you two have afternoon tea on the porch swing?" Owen says.

"Excuse me. This is a sucker."

Everest reaches across me and smacks Lucas on the back of his head. "You could have told us you were taking a break."

"Why would I do that? I was hoping you would be finished by the time our break was over."

"You'll have to pay me a lot more than just pizza for that."

"Speaking of pizza," Lucas says, lifting his phone and checking the time. "Andi should be here any minute with them. I'm going to get a few more boxes unloaded out of the truck before it gets here."

"Oh sure. Now that we've sat down," Owen teases.

Lucas is slow getting up from the bench and I can barely muzzle my groan as I follow him. On my third trip out to the truck for a box of God knows what, an animal running behind Lucas's house catches my eye.

"Was that a bear?"

"I'm not sure. All I saw was a black blur." Lucas and I take a few cautious steps when a fluffy black dog comes running from around the corner. "Holy shit."

"I'm sorry," a guy yells from the driveway. "That's my dog. He got out of the fence." The only neighbor close to Lucas and Tana's large property lives across the street.

"No worries. We'll help you catch him," Lucas says.

As Lucas, his neighbor, and I are chasing this damn dog all around the yard, Andi pulls into the driveway and steps out of her car with the pizzas in a stack in one hand and a bag of soda in the other. The dog bolts in her direction, and she squeals as it jumps right into her car and sits in the passenger seat. "You either like that I smell like pizza, or you really like car rides."

"Don't worry, he's friendly," the neighbor shouts as we all jog toward her car.

Lucas gets to Andi first and takes the pizza and two liters from her. She smiles at me, and then her eyes get wide as she takes in Lucas's neighbor next to me.

"Oh my God. Bobby?"

"No way. Andrea?"

Andi squeals again and hugs the man next to me. "What are you doing here? Aren't you living in Wyoming?"

"I am. Just here visiting my aunt."

"Mason, this is Bobby. Bobby, meet Mason. Bobby and I know each other from way back. He used to help my grandma, and we'd hang out when I came to visit in the summers.

"And this is?" Andi points to the big, fluffy dog sitting in her passenger seat.

"That's Leon. He's just a big, dumb baby who likes to jump the fence when he sees a rabbit."

A brush fire engulfs my insides as I watch them laugh and reminisce. Every time his hand grazes her forearm, I want to explode into a thousand pieces and cover her body. I don't know why, but I really fucking hate him touching her.

"Come on and eat," Lucas shouts from the porch. "You're welcome to join us…"

"Bobby. The name's Bobby, and I appreciate that, but I have to figure out how to get him back home without his leash. I wish I could guarantee that he won't do this again while I'm in town, but that would make me a liar."

"It's no big deal. Stop on by anytime."

"I'll do that."

Bobby moves to Andi's passenger door and tries to pry Leon out of the seat, but he's not budging.

"Why don't I just drive you and Leon up to your aunt's house?"

"That would be great. Sorry to bother you."

"No bother. C'mon, hop in."

Bobby gets in the back seat of Andi's car, and she must see the hatred I've developed for a man I don't even know in the last two minutes. She walks up to me and places her hand on my jaw, stroking it with her thumb. "You should really try to relax this jaw more often. Eventually, you won't be able to open your mouth anymore."

"How's your first pizza night going?" I ask her, desperate to change the subject and irritated that she could see the jealousy on my face.

"It's insane. I can barely keep up, which is why I have to hurry back to the diner. I think every house in Cresna ordered pizza tonight."

"So, this Bobby is a good guy?"

"You don't like him, do you?"

"I don't know him. But I don't like what my gut is telling me."

"Well, tell your gut not to worry. He's just a friend." She turns to open her car door and pauses before she opens it. "And not like our version of friends. So don't go there."

I nod because it's all I can bring myself to do as she gets in. Pretending to head inside, I walk to the porch, turn around, and watch her leave Lucas's driveway and pull into the one across the street. Because of all the trees surround the two properties, her car disappears.

"Are you coming?" Lucas says with a full mouth through the screen door. "What the hell are you doing?"

Andi's car appears again as she exits Bobby's driveway and turns down the road that leads to Cresna. "Yep, I'm coming."

"Wow. I know I said I'd let it go, but you've got it bad, brother."

"Just wanted to make sure she got out all right."

Lucas rolls his eyes and opens the screen door for me, and I head inside.

After the pizza is gone and we've sat around for an extra half hour, we peel ourselves off the couch that's placed in the middle of the living room and get the last boxes out of the truck. The one I grab happens to be another box for Iris's room. Her door is closed when I walk up to it, and I can hear little sobs from inside. I knock, and her little feet pad fast across the floor and the door opens.

"Hey, Piglet. What's the matter?"

I pity the first boy that draws a tear from this child's eye. "I lost Mason," she wails, and more tears fall down her already tear-soaked cheeks. She climbs up on her bed and dangles her tiny feet over the edge.

"I'm right here." I set the box down and sit next to her, wrapping my arm around her shoulder.

"Not you, Uncle Mason. The other Mason."

This could be tricky. Ever since I pulled Tana's daughter out of the car when they went into the ditch, she's been my little piglet, and I've been the fun uncle I never thought I'd get to be since I have no siblings. She's also decided to name every single stuffed animal she has Mason.

I start opening boxes and pulling out stuffed animals. "Is it elephant Mason?"

Her breath hiccups, and it's the cutest and saddest thing I've ever seen. "No."

"Hippopotamus Mason?"

She shakes her head, and I break through the tape on the box I just brought in. Sitting on top is a bright white polar bear. I pull it out, and she shrieks.

"Mason! You found Mason, Uncle Mason. Thank you." She jumps off the bed and runs to me, grabbing it from my hand. She throws her arms up, I lift her, and she hugs me as tight as she can. "I love you, Uncle Mason."

"Love you too, Piglet."

Tana clears her throat from behind me, and Iris wiggles in my arms. "Mommy, look. Mason. We found him." I set her down, and her pigtails bounce as she runs out of the room.

"She's lucky to have you," Tana says as I pick up the other stuffed animals that got thrown onto the floor in our hunt.

"I'm going to remind you of those words when she's a teenager and she likes me more than you."

Tana laughs. "That's when I'll appreciate you even more for giving her a safe place to run to." I chuckle, and she leans against the wall. "You're going to make a great dad someday, Mason."

A cold rush flows through my veins. "I don't think that's going to happen. I'm just happy to have the uncle title."

"You really don't think you'll ever have kids?"

I shake my head. "Nope. Never going to happen."

She takes a big breath and blows it out slowly. "If that's really what you want."

"What I want doesn't matter."

"What does that mean?"

"Nothing. I shouldn't have said that. I'm just overtired, I think."

Tana nods and pushes away from the wall. "I know you are. I'm so thankful you helped us out today. Tomorrow won't be nearly so bad. Just unpacking the boxes, so if you need to stay home, we've got it covered over here."

"I'll be here tomorrow."

I'll never forget the first time I met Tana after the car accident. Her smile was the first thing I noticed. It shows her kind and pure heart. Sometimes, strangers turn into family. And I couldn't have gotten luckier finding this one. I haven't talked to anyone about my past, and I just got real close to telling Tana all about it.

"I'm sure Iris will be happy to have you here tomorrow. Maybe you can help her organize all her Masons on the shelves."

We both laugh, and I rest my arm over her shoulders as we walk out to the living room together.

"I'm going to head out," I say. "What time do you want me to be here in the morning?"

"That depends. Are you coming from your house or someone else's?" Lucas asks with a smirk.

"Give me a time, or I'm showing up at eight tomorrow night."

"I need a little sleep, so how about ten?"

"Thank God. I'll see you then."

Iris runs up and hugs my leg. "Bye, Uncle Mason."

"See you tomorrow, Piglet."

She smiles wide and runs into the other room. The cool evening air hits me as I walk out of the house and into my car. I give Bobby's aunt's driveway a bold stare as I pull out of Tana and Lucas's and head toward Cresna. I can't stop myself from looking in the windows of the diner, just hoping to get a glimpse of Andi as I pass by. I also can't stop the disappointment inside when I don't see her.

As I pull into my own driveway and look at my dark and empty house, it hits me how close I came to letting it all out with Tana. It's not that I don't want them to have the information. Reliving it all sounds almost as much of a nightmare as going through it. And I'll avoid that as long as I possibly can. For my own sake.

CHAPTER SIX

Andi

THE FIRST PIZZA night was better than I could have expected. We were slammed all night. And even though everyone was exhausted by closing time, there were smiles all around. Probably due to only having to work until noon tomorrow and having Monday off. Most of the crew at the diner have been here for years, and getting any day of the weekend off was difficult. But that's when most important things happen in life. Birthday parties. Sunday dinner. Taking the kids to the park in the center of town. I feel in my soul closing the diner early on Sundays and all day on Mondays was the right decision.

I park in the driveway, turn my car off, and stare at my little white ranch home. Scared. Mason isn't here tonight, which means it's the first night I have to face being alone in the house. Knowing someone was inside feels so invasive. So violating. I'm just glad nothing was stolen, but at the same time, that doesn't make any sense. The longer I sit in my car, the more anger replaces the fear. *Absolutely not, Andrea. Do not let someone else do this to you.* Refusing to let some asshole taint the tranquility of my home, I grab my purse, get out of the car, and walk up to my house.

With my key in the door, I turn the handle and hesitate when my grandma's voice fills my head. *"Don't worry about being strong. Focus on being brave. You can build strength as long as you're brave enough to find shelter while you do it. I will always be your shelter."* Feeling her strength, I push open the door and go inside. So what if I have to flip on every single light in the house. So what if I check the locks on the door three times before I go to bed. So what if I leave the TV on in the living room so there's noise in the house while I try to go to bed. There's power in realizing none of those things make me weak, and eventually, I get strong enough to fall asleep.

RING! Still half-unconscious, I jump out of bed, hit my knee on the nightstand, and stub my toe while trying to find my phone in the dark. The light from the screen blinds me as I blink to see who's calling. My heart sinks when I realize it's my alarm company for the diner.

"Hello?"

"Hi. This is Claire with PPA Security. We got a signal that your alarm is going off at 15 Main Street. Is everything okay, or should we dispatch police?"

Panic hits my stomach. "That's my restaurant, and I'm not there. Please have the police go."

"Confirmed the police are now notified. Would you like me to stay on the phone with you until they arrive?"

"No. Thank you."

"We're always here if you need further assistance."

I hang up, run into the kitchen, grab my purse and keys, shove my shoes on, and run out the door. In this town, there's only one police officer, but the county police office is located between Pine Valley and Birkenshire. So when things go down, Tucker will call for assistance, but the other officers are coming from far away. So sometimes when you need a cop, you can wait a long time to get a response. Especially if Tucker isn't on shift. It's very possible I could drive to the diner only to face whatever set my alarm off on my own.

I start my car and text Mason.

ANDI: Are you awake?

What a stupid question. It's four in the morning. I bite my lip until it hurts but release it as soon as I see those three bouncing dots.

MASON: I am now.

ANDI: My alarm is going off at the diner. I hate to ask, but do you think you could meet me there?

I'm out of my driveway and halfway down the street before he texts back.

MASON: Already in the car.

Thankfully, Tucker's police car is already parked at the diner as I pull in. He gives me a nod as I park and get out.

"It looks like…"

Screeching tires interrupt him, and both of our heads turn as Mason flies into the parking lot.

"Would you look at that," Tucker says as Mason shoots out of his car, shirt in his hands, jeans barely hanging on to his hips, work boots untied. If I wasn't so worried about what's going on with the diner right now, I would have a hard time keeping the drool in my mouth.

He walks past Tucker and doesn't stop until he's within reach of me. A large warm hand covers my arm as he bends his head and looks into my eyes.

"Are you okay?"

"I'm fine. I just got here."

"What happened?"

Tucker clears his throat and takes a step toward us. "I was just about to tell her. It doesn't seem like anyone got into the place. But they sure found the biggest doggone rock they could and threw it right through the door."

"Oh no." I cover my face with my hands. "Why? Why would someone do this?"

Tucker's radio makes a loud noise, and he puts his finger up and walks a few feet away.

"It's just glass. We'll fix it. Probably just some kids being stupid with homecoming next weekend."

"They got the hardware store too," Tucker shouts. "Same thing. Rock through the window."

"See? I'd bet my money..." Mason freezes as I pull my elbows in further, trying to warm myself. His eyes travel down my body, and the corner of his jaw ticks. He glares at Tucker and back at me, then walks to his car and starts digging inside. He pulls out a big hooded sweatshirt and shakes it out a few times before walking back to me and putting it over my head. It drapes like an oversized blanket on my body and fits me like a dress coming halfway down my thighs.

"Not that you don't look good in those pajamas. I just don't think you'd appreciate the whole town checking out your ass hanging out of them."

"I wouldn't appreciate it? Or you wouldn't?"

"If we're being honest with each other, I would say both."

I wish I had more control over my own damn lips. They seem to smile whenever the hell they want to around Mason. "Well, thank you. It's much warmer, that's for sure."

"Do you even own other pajamas?"

"Of course," I say, scrunching up my nose, then wickedly grinning. "But I definitely can't be in public with those."

His jaw drops, and I revel in the exact response I was hoping for. He reaches for my hip, but Tucker walks back up to us.

"I checked all the doors, and they're all still locked, but I could see the rock inside. Do you have cameras here?" Tucker asks.

"I do, but only inside. The outside ones got messed up with the storm."

"They'll probably be no help, then, but I'd like to see them. I'll have you unlock the door, and I'll do a quick look around just to make sure everything inside is secure, and then if it's okay with you, I'd like to run down to Murphy's Hardware and see if his cameras picked up anything."

"Of course. Let me grab my keys and purse from the car." I left my purse and everything in the car when I pulled up. Things might be getting a little ridiculous around town, but I figured they would be safe since the cop was right here with me. As I walk to the car, I'm not sure what Mason and Tucker are talking about, but they both keep flashing their eyes in my direction. I grab my keys from the ignition, walk back to the guys, and hold them out. Both reach for them, but Mason takes them first and spins around, stomping toward the diner's glass door.

Tucker shakes his head and smirks at me.

"We're just friends, Tucker."

"Oh I know. And I'm just here deliverin' the mail." He makes a clicking sound with his mouth as he winks, then jogs to the door as Mason pushes it open. I follow them into the diner as Mason and Tucker flip on the lights.

"Careful," Mason says, meeting me at the doorway. The glass crunches under his feet as he wraps one arm around my waist and lifts me off the ground and places me back down away from the shards. The beeping from the alarm gets louder as I walk toward Tucker, and he opens the back storage room where the panel is.

"You can shut this off now, Andi. The back door is secure, and I don't see anything else suspicious."

I punch in the code and hold my hand out to Mason. He puts the keys in my hand, and I open my office. Everything is just how

I left it last night. Letting my purse fall from my shoulder, it makes a thud on the desk. My bare thighs hit the cold leather of my office chair, and I rub my eyes.

Tucker pats Mason on the shoulder. "You gonna stay here with her while I run over to Murphy's?"

"I don't answer dumb questions, Tuck."

"Apparently, neither does Andi," Tucker says, teasing me about Mason.

Mason squishes his eyebrows together and opens his mouth to say something, but two car doors shutting in the parking lot stops him. Tucker touches his hand to his belt as he turns to walk out of the office.

"It's just a friend of mine, Tuck." Tucker stops when we hear a voice call for Mason.

"You called Lucas?"

"I see you've got this covered for now. Andi, if you could pull up the camera footage just in case, I'll be back to look at it as soon as I can."

I nod, and as Tucker walks out, Lucas walks in, followed by Owen and Everest.

"You guys didn't have to come. Everything is fine," I say, feeling guilty that they're here at this time of the morning.

"We brought plywood to close up your door until you get it fixed. What the fuck happened?" Lucas asks.

Mason goes to speak, but the weight of all of this has just grown too heavy, and I start to break. "Oh, you know. The usual. Open doors, broken glass, and the random feelings that someone is watching me. Just a regular goddamn day in my life." I slam my elbows onto the desk and lean my face into my hands. "Sorry, I'm just overstressed, overtired, and overwhelmed. You guys don't need to hear about this shit."

"Hold the fuck up," Mason says, putting his hand up. "What

do you mean you feel like someone is watching you? You never told me that."

"I'm sure it happens to everyone at some point. I'm just on edge after my front door incident."

"No. It doesn't, Andi. Explain."

There's that look again on Mason's face. The one that looks like he could rip someone in half. And there are two more men standing in front of me that all have that same look.

"I don't know. When I opened yesterday, I just got this strange feeling that someone else was around, but Brice didn't come in for thirty minutes after that."

"Was that it?" Everest asks.

"No. I got an eerie feeling the other day when I was walking to my car to go to Tana's house. And another one when I walked into my bedroom. I swear, I'm probably just being paranoid."

Mason's jaw ticks faster than I've ever seen it, and if I had to guess, he's grinding his teeth inside those pursed lips. The men behind him don't look any happier.

"Boys, we need to talk," Mason says, never taking his eyes from me. Lucas, Everest, and Owen walk out of my office, and Mason puts his fists on the desk and leans over it, getting so close to my face I can smell his aftershave.

"You work on pulling up that footage, and I'll take care of the rest."

"What does that mean?"

"It means I've got to talk to my boys."

Mason walks out, and my heart beats in my throat. He didn't think I was overtired. He didn't think the stress from all of this could just be causing a little more paranoia. No. Mason believes that my feelings are legit. And now, I'm more freaked-out than ever.

CHAPTER SEVEN

MASON

I'VE COME to the conclusion that staying out of this diner was the best thing I could have done for myself after the wedding. That is, if I wanted to keep my head on straight about Andi. During the past week, my head is not only twisted, it's been spun around and knocked right off my damn shoulders.

"What can I get you two today?" Tana asks, leaning her hip into Lucas's arm. "Brice is trying out his new chili recipe for the Fall Fest this weekend. It's so good."

"I'll have that," Lucas says.

"Me too."

"Comin' right up," Tana says and walks away.

Andi catches my eye as she comes out of the kitchen and jogs to the ringing phone by the register. The looks Andi shoots me as she moves around the diner, doing whatever it is owners of a restaurant do, drive me crazy. One of these days, it's going to get me in trouble. And by trouble, I mean taking her ass in that office of hers, shutting the door, and showing her what all of her sexy side smirks do to me. What they make me want to do to her.

It's been a few days since the rock flew through the door of the diner. Lucas and I have been in every day for lunch. The door was fixed yesterday by one of our business acquaintances from Birkenshire, who owns a glass business. He owed me a favor and put one hell of a rush on getting this glass replaced. The diner looks like nothing ever happened. I have a lot of those kinds of people in my life. I don't have a lot of friends outside of my circle, but I have a lot of business contacts and people I'm friendly with. Friends are people you'd trust with your life, and after what I've been through, trust isn't something I just give away.

It's also why we're watching out for Andi. I don't trust people, and if she feels like she's being watched, after the door and the rock, I'm not taking any chances. I've seen some crazy, scary shit happen in little towns. It happens everywhere. And if someone is messing with Andi, they're going to get the shock of a lifetime when they come for her and get us instead.

Everest is shipping me the best security cameras for Andi's house and for outside of the diner. Owen is on standby in case I need him to locate someone or find out pretty much anything. He's a genius on the computer and can hack almost anything, but since he's a good guy, he only does it if it helps someone. It's scary the things he can find out about people, and I don't have the first clue how he does it. I'm just glad he's on my side.

As for me and Lucas, we're paying close attention to everything that is going on in town. We're watching everyone. Especially after the cameras at Murphy's picked up the image of a person throwing the rock at his window. It wasn't teenage kids. If only people in this town took their security a little more seriously, we'd have more than a blurred-out shadow figure. I'm pretty sure his cameras were from 1990.

Andi's curvy hips shimmy as she walks toward our booth. I lick my dry lips, and her eyes drop to them as she stops in front of me. "Hey, guys."

"Everything going all right today?" Lucas asks, as he always does.

"Yep. Going great." I slide across the booth, and Andi sits down next to me. It was a mistake. Her sweet vanilla scent hits my nose, and all I want to do is bury my face into her neck and breathe her in. Instead, I take a drink of my sweet tea and act like none of those thoughts are running through my head.

"I should be getting those cameras delivered today. I can install them tonight if that's okay with you."

"Oh yeah, that'd be great. I hate not having cameras in the back of the diner. That storm really messed things up around here. I think I'll feel better once they're up."

"I'll come hook the cameras up here first, and then I'll head to your house to hook up the others."

Tana walks up holding a brown serving tray with bowls, bread, and crackers. "I'll talk to you later," Andi says to me. "Bye, Lucas." He waves to Andi as Tana sets the bowls in front of us, and Lucas's eyes get wide.

"Here you go, boys. Brice is insisting you let him know what you think."

"There's bacon in this chili?" he asks, looking giddy as a schoolboy. He pulls the one long strip that was half in the chili and holds it up. "This better be good." He takes a bite and smacks the table. "Tell him it's the best chili I've ever had."

"Lucas. You haven't even tasted the chili yet," Tana says.

"Is there more bacon in it?"

"There's little pieces mixed in too."

"Then I don't need to. The bacon is perfect, which apparently is harder to do than I thought." Tana rolls her eyes, and Lucas takes a big bite of the chili. "Told you. This is the shit. Tell him. It's the best."

Tana laughs and walks to another table to check on them. Andi crosses the diner again, and I can't stop following her with my eyes. I'm annoyed at how much she captivates me just by existing.

Lucas's spoon hits his bowl, and the loud clank draws my attention to him. "When are you going to admit it?"

"Oh Jesus. We're going back to this again, aren't we?"

"Yes. This again. This forever until you just stop being an idiot and make yourself happy for once. In all the time I've known you, never have I seen you genuinely happy. Especially not with a woman."

"I told you before. There's something wrong with me. When Zeena moved out, I didn't even care. What kind of monster feels like that after a relationship? It's like I'm incapable of having emotions."

"Brother, I've been there. I get it. You don't want to get hurt, so you stop yourself from feeling anything."

"It's not me I'm worried about. I don't want to hurt her."

He smirks. "I can already tell you'd never let that happen."

"Exactly. That's why we're friends."

I can sense her near before ever laying my eyes on her. She walks to the table adjacent to us, and like dowsing rods to water, I turn my head toward her. Andi smiles at the people in the booth, hands them what looks like a gift certificate, and returns to the register. Once I bring my eyes back to Lucas, he's staring at me. No smile or joking expression. Just his rigid, straight face.

"Brother," he says. "You are not friends."

Fuck.

———

Lucas let me take off early since it was almost six o'clock and his other right-hand man, Lenny, showed up at our jobsite. Lenny took over for me so I could come to the diner and get these cameras up and rolling. I pull into the back lot of the diner and park next to Andi's car. The leaves crunch under my feet as I round the trunk to grab the box of equipment from the passenger seat. But a small, neon-colored paper stuck to the back door of the diner catches my attention.

As I read each word, my palms sweat and my blood turns to a flow of lava.

I HATE YOU

I was hoping my gut feeling was off and someone wasn't targeting Andi and the restaurant. It's still not lost on me that this note could be for anyone working in the diner. But that doesn't stop the anger growing inside. I shove the sticky note into my pocket and run inside the diner to make sure Andi is all right.

She isn't in the dining room, so I jog to her office, but it's empty. I check the waitress's hallway before running into the kitchen.

"Yo, what's up, Mason?" Brice says, taken aback that I've just barged into the kitchen.

"Have you seen Andi?"

"Yeah, she speed walked past me a few minutes ago."

"Question for you. Have you pissed anyone off lately?"

"Only every day of my life." He shrugs. "It's a gift."

"Anyone that would throw a rock through the door of the diner?"

He stops moving around the sliced steak on the grill. "My ex-wife is petty and vindictive as hell. She fucking hates me, but I think she'd set my house on fire before throwing rocks into the diner's window."

"Do me a favor and let me know if you see anything or anyone odd around here."

"Will do." The sound of his metal spatula scraping against the grill gives me the chills.

I take a deep breath, knowing that this note could be aimed toward Brice or anyone else in here. Rhonda walks into the kitchen and leans against the wall.

"Lord forgive me. I don't like to talk badly about people, but that little girl that just sat down at my table is the spawn of Satan himself. Bless her heart."

Brice laughs, and I turn to Rhonda.

"Have you seen Andi?"

"Last I saw her, she was takin' a small bag of trash out to the dumpster. Actually, she's been gone a few minutes now. Wonder what's takin' her so long."

My heart starts to pound against my chest as I scan the dining room for her long brunette hair. My muscles get twitchy when I don't see her by the register either. I'm about to run out the door to the dumpster that sits on the back corner when she comes walking out of the hallway that leads to her office. I move my feet faster than my normal walking pace until I reach her.

"Are you okay?"

Her eyebrows furrow. "Yes," she says cautiously. "Is something wrong?"

For a second, I think about showing her the paper I found stuck to the back door. But remembering how scared she was the other night, I stop before my fingers ever touch the paper in my pocket. "Everything is fine. I just came in to tell you I was getting started on the cameras out back, and I couldn't find you. My mind just went somewhere dark for a second."

She places her hands on my arms. "I'm fine. I was in the bathroom, if you must know. I'll text you next time." A playful grin crosses her face, and I want nothing more than to kiss her lips. Her flirting and gentle touch stoke the sparks that ignite when she's around. She wants me just as much as I want her. If only there was a way to erase my past and give in to her.

"I've got to get back to help Jessica. I let Tana go home to Iris since Lucas is working late. Do you want something to eat or anything?"

"Thanks, I'm good. I'll be in the back if you need me."

She nods, and I hate when she takes her hands off me and moves away. It feels like I just went from a Florida summer to Alaska's winter. When she disappears into the kitchen, I turn to walk out but feel someone's eyes on me. Sitting in the booth in the far corner of the diner is Zeena, and she's waving me over.

I don't want to rehash things with Zeena. But I can't help but wonder what the hell she's doing here. Last I knew, she moved in with her sister in Colbert, which is over an hour away. I walk across the dining room and glance over my shoulder, making sure that Andi hasn't come out of the kitchen yet. I couldn't give a shit about Zeena, but I don't want Andi to assume I'm talking to another woman. Truth is, the only woman I have any interest in talking to is Andi.

"What are you doing here, Zeena?"

"Wow. That's how you're going to greet me? Geez. I was going to say that it's good to see you and that I miss you, but now that you've opened your mouth, I'm thinking I don't."

"Good. What are you doing here?"

"I've been spending the week with Dusty. You know I have people I care about in this town other than you."

"Another good thing to hear. One person shouldn't be someone's entire world."

"You know, that's just your problem. You refuse to accept your own heart. I know you loved me, you just…"

Zeena still doesn't get it. I never loved her. That was the problem. "Did you need something? Otherwise, I've got more important shit to do than stand here and argue with you over a relationship that ended a long time ago."

I feel her in my bones before her hand wraps around my arm. "I'm not trying to get involved here," Andi says in a whisper. "But can the two of you lower your voices a bit. You're disturbing the other diners."

Zeena aims her dagger eyes at Andi's hand on my arm, and I cover it with mine.

"I'm sorry, babe," I whisper.

"You're dating a waitress?" she shrieks. "Oh, that's rich. You bouncing from woman to woman is one thing. But to go as low as a desperate waitress in this shitty little diner is surprising. Even for you." She moves her eyes to Andi. "Beware of this asshole, honey. He'll use you, spit you out, and step on your remains on his way to his next ho."

I open my mouth to say something, but Andi beats me to it. "Actually, I own this diner, and you can take your entitled, rude, and bitchy self out of my restaurant. Don't ever step foot in here again, or I'll direct my staff to have you removed. And if you talk about Mason that way again, I'll make your eye match your black, fake designer shoes."

Zeena's mouth isn't the only one hanging wide open. I grab Andi's arm to stop her from getting closer and closer to Zeena.

"Real professional for a business owner," Zeena says, standing from the booth just as her friend shows up. "We're leaving. Someone isn't aware of who she's with yet, and she's still defending him." She hauls her purse over her shoulder. "I remember when I was still stupid enough to do that too."

"Apparently you're still pretty stupid because you haven't left yet, and my country is about to show itself. Get out of my restaurant."

With my hand still firmly holding on to Andi, we watch Zeena and her friend casually waltz out of the diner.

Andi turns to me, a gleam in her eye. "An ex of yours? She's lovely."

I grab her hand, holding it tightly, and pull her across the dining room, past the register, down the hall, and into her office. I kick the door shut with my foot as I press her hard against the wall. She sharply inhales as I close my mouth on hers and thrust my tongue inside. She tightens her grip on my arms as she pulls, demanding that my body get closer to hers.

I need this woman. The way she just defended me and stood her ground was the sexiest thing I've ever seen. Her tongue glides with fervor over mine, kissing me hard and deep while our hands travel over each other's body, frantic for the static between us to turn into a lightning bolt of passion. Breaking our kiss, I graze my teeth over her jaw before running my tongue down her neck and hear the door lock before her hand touches my jaw. She moans and calls my name with a hunger I haven't heard before. I pause, feeling each letter of my name punch me in the chest.

"You should listen to her," I whisper against her ear.

"What?" she pants.

"I am an asshole."

"Just shut up, Mason," she says, reaching between us and taking my erection in her hand.

I nearly swallow my tongue and untuck her white shirt out of her long, navy pencil skirt. All sense of control is gone as she strokes me, and my hands fly over her body, not able to get enough of her. I pull her away from the wall, never losing her kiss until I back her up against the desk.

Her hooded, blue eyes sink into mine. "Hurry," she pants. One word is all it takes. I spin her around, pressing her chest down onto the desk. I lift her skirt up over her ass and tug her panties down. Her stifled giggle fuels my excitement. I run my fingers over her soaking core and rush to free myself from my pants. I grab a condom from my wallet, roll it on, and work into her. A long low groan comes from her as she grips the sides of the desk and I bury myself inside Andi.

"Damn, baby," I say, breathless.

"There's no time," she whispers, reaching behind her, pulling on my thighs, and sinking me in as deep as I can go. "Fast, hard, and quiet."

Dear God. This woman is trying to kill me. I pull slowly out against her wishes and then plunge hard into her, relishing the way her ass jiggles every time our skin connects. The noises coming from her as I pick up pace, thrusting and digging my fingers into her curvy hips, are enough to toss my ass right over that cliff. Her ponytail bounces, teasing me. I grab it with one hand and pull, causing her shoulders to come off the desk as I slam into her.

"Andi?" My body stills as Rhonda calls through the door.

She tries to clear her throat, but I know there's nothing in there to clear. "Yeah?"

"Table six is asking to speak to you."

I grin and move slowly out of her, knowing she can't react. "I'll...I'll be right there. I'm on a phone call." She practically yells at poor Rhonda. I slowly push back inside and just as slowly pull back out.

"Okay, doll." I slam into her, and she shoves part of her shirt into her mouth as I continue to thrust, hard and deep. "I'll let them know you'll be a moment. 'Cause you're on a phone call."

"Thank you," she blurts out as I feel her start to convulse around my dick. Thank God. I can't hold back anymore either. I let her hair go, grip her hips, and watch as I bring her to orgasm. Her muffled whimpers, white knuckles gripping the sides of the desk, and trembling thighs send me over the edge. A few more fast and hard thrusts, and I bury myself deep inside of her, groaning with my own release.

I've never felt like this. No woman has ever taken charge of me. I've always been in charge. Always able to control myself, hold back, and make hard decisions. But when I'm around Andi, all of those things get thrown out of a window. How does she do this to me? I grunt as if pulling out of her is excruciating. It only is because I want to stay buried in her for hours. Feel her pulsing core against me. I kiss her shoulder, and she flips around.

"Oh my God. That was amazing." She bends down, pulls up her underwear, pushes the bottom of her skirt down, and quickly tucks her shirt back in. "Jesus. I feel like I can't walk. How the hell am I going to get through work the next few hours?"

I grab a tissue from her desk, clean myself off, and put the leftover evidence of the best sex I've ever had into the trash can. She removes the elastic and threads her fingers through her just-fucked hair as she smiles at me. I wrap my arm around her waist, pull her to me, and kiss her. It never feels like enough.

"I have to go," she says. "Are you coming over tonight?"

"Yep. I have to put the cameras up."

The slightest jolt of her head catches my attention. "Right," she says. "The cameras. I'm so lucky to have a friend like you." She presses another quick kiss to my lips, then runs out of the office. But I can't seem to move my feet. I didn't like how those words just came out of her mouth. When she jerked, it was like something hit her in the face, and I really fucking hate it. I've never been more sure of what I want in my whole life. I just don't know how to make myself believe that I can have it.

———

"You're all set up," I say, standing on Andi's front porch. "Just pull up that app on your phone when you want to check the cameras or look around outside."

"Thank you so much for getting these up for me. Are you hungry? I brought some chicken home from the diner for us."

As much as I want to go inside and pretend that this hesitation isn't building inside of me, I can't do it to her. I'm already hurting her by taking things too far.

"I can't" is all I muster up. "I'm sorry, but this has…"

Her face doesn't flinch like I thought it would. Her eyes don't fill with the sadness I was dreading would appear in them. "It's okay," she says, shaking her head. "You made your intentions clear in the beginning."

"You did too." The look on her face as she nods in agreement shows no emotion. It makes me wonder if I would have been the one hurt. Again.

"I want to be your friend, Andi. I'm not going anywhere. But I think for the sake of both of us, we need to drop the benefits part of it."

She crosses her arms as she casually leans against the door. "Probably should have never started. But today…I don't regret today." We both smile wide.

"Me either. If you need me for anything, call me."

She nods, and I walk down the steps. "Mason?"

I freeze, praying she's about to stop me from leaving. "Is it me?" Her words feel like a hot knife slicing through my organs.

"What?"

"Nothing. Good night, Mason."

"Good night." I stand for a few moments looking at the light filtering through the glass of her front door. *What the hell does she mean by that?*

CHAPTER EIGHT

Andi

IT'S BEEN A FEW DAYS, but every time I sit at this desk, all I think about is Mason. I can almost feel his hand in my hair and the heat between us. We made an agreement. And I botched it. I let my heart open up, knowing damn well misery would come flooding in. It usually does. Except Mason didn't do anything wrong. I knew the terms, but the truth is, I was glad when he stepped back. The sex we had on this desk was fast and furious. But it was also full of emotion and magnified the pull he has on me.

A knock on my office door makes me scream, and I put my hand over my racing heart.

"Sorry, Andi," Brice says. "We got the croutons in for the chili, right?"

"Yeah. They should be in the stockroom."

"I checked there. Twice. I can't find them."

Brice and I exchange a worried glance, and I shoot out of my chair. "What?" I march past him and straight into the stockroom. Brice walks in behind me, and we start looking over all of the supplies. The special croutons that Brice requested for the chili we're serving at Fall Fest tomorrow night are not anywhere in sight. I start grabbing things and flinging them to other shelves.

"What are you doing?"

"They have to be here. I ordered them."

I start throwing more things, desperate to find these fucking croutons. I've made an absolute disaster out of five shelves, and I'm on the brink of tears before Brice stops me.

"Andrea. It's not that important. I can do without them."

"I ordered them," I say, marching out of the stockroom and back to my desk. I pull up my account with the food distributor, ready to complain about not getting an item I ordered, but I don't find the croutons on my order. "Brice, I'm so sorry. I didn't order them. I must have had them up on my screen and then never actually placed the order. This is my fault. I'm sorry."

"No big deal. It's just a topping. We'd be in trouble if it was the tomatoes or beans, but we're all good. Everything else is ready to go for tomorrow, so don't worry."

I fake a smile and nod.

"Andrea. It's just croutons."

He taps my doorframe twice and smiles, then walks out of view. To him it might just be the croutons. To me, it's a sign I'm distracted. This diner is all I have, and Brice might not be upset I forgot his croutons this time, but what happens if it's something bigger next time? It's a good thing Mason decided to pour water on our heated *friendship*. I can't focus around him.

———

THE TOWN LIGHTS UP with the most beautiful orange glow as music streams through the sky. The tents have orange lights strung all around with colorful leaf garland. Large bulb string lights are strung from each booth to the stage, where the band is set up, filling the area with a warm ambiance. The fest consists of a band and a dance floor, a beer tent, the diner's food tent, a few crafters tents, and, best of all, Josephine's dessert tent. She makes the best pumpkin pie in the world. Fall Fest is the one time of year when everyone comes out to the small park in town to dance, eat, and mingle. We especially needed it this year after that horrible storm blew through. Lucas and Mason are still trying to get caught up on the jobs they have in town.

"Wow," Leslie, Tana's mom, says, standing next to me with a mouth full of chili. "This is incredible."

"I would never want to lose Brice, but sometimes, I wonder why he isn't living in some big city, running his own kitchen."

Brice clears his throat from behind us. "That constant fast-paced life isn't for me. I like it here just fine."

"Selfishly, I'm glad to hear that," I say.

Tana and Iris walk back to us from the bathrooms on the side of the park. "Mama, if you want to stay, Lucas will bring you home since he drove his truck here. I've got to go though. She's already met her quota for sugar-rushed temper tantrums today. If I don't get her to bed soon, I'm going to send her home with Mason."

Leslie and I laugh. "I'm about ready too."

"Lucas," Tana calls across two tents.

My body starts to tingle as I feel Mason getting near. I've managed to avoid him these last few days. He and Lucas came into the diner for lunch, but I pretended to be busy in my office. Mostly, I was just in there wishing he'd bust through the door and take me on the desk again.

Tana steps aside and talks to Lucas while Mason steps closer to me. "Hey," he says, shoving his hands into his pockets.

"Hey."

"Everything going okay?"

"Yep."

"Lucas and I will be coming this week to get that roof fixed. Sorry it's taken us so long."

"You guys have been so busy. I appreciate whenever you can get there as long as the roof doesn't start leaking."

"It won't. I've already checked and readjusted the tarps a few times."

"You have?" I have no idea when Mason had the time to recheck the tarps at the diner. According to Tana, they've been working so hard.

"Hey, Mason," Lucas calls. "Can you help me real quick? Tana bought a damn side table, and it's awkward to carry to her car by myself."

"I'd love to help you," Mason teases, bringing a laugh out of me. And then, his smile fades as he looks over my shoulder. "Great," he huffs.

I turn around as Zeena walks up to Josephine's tent. "Don't let her get to you."

"She just seems to suddenly be popping up everywhere. She used to tell me how much she hated Cresna, so I'm surprised she's sticking around so much."

"C'mon, Mason," Lucas says, pulling us from the conversation. "Let's get this done so grouchy pants here can go to bed."

"Better go help him," he says. "You'll be around tonight?"

"Yep."

"Good. Tana drove herself so Lucas is going to stay for a while with me. But I'll come look for you in a little while."

I'm not sure if that's a good thing or a bad thing. I lean against the table in our tent, not exactly sure what to do with myself.

"Why don't you go get a drink or something," Brice says.

"I don't want to leave if you need me here."

"Jessica just ran to the diner to grab more napkins, and we'll be fine the rest of the night. Go relax a little bit and, I don't know, maybe have a little fun."

It's not easy for me to take Brice's advice, but I force myself to. As I walk across the park to the beer tent, I nod and smile at everyone I pass, and I get the same in return. It's one of the things I missed so much when I lived in Wisconsin. Not like people there weren't friendly. It's just different in a small town where everyone knows who you are. I lean up against the bar, which is made of long pieces of plywood.

"Hey, Andi. What can I get you?"

"Hi, Arthur. I'll take a hard seltzer, please."

"Comin' up."

I turn to my right and see Mr. Murphy, who owns the hardware store. He was also really close to my grandma. "Hey, Mr. Murphy. Did you get that window fixed?"

A friendly smile spreads across his face as one of his bushy white eyebrows raises. "I did. Mason and Lucas hooked me up with the same man who fixed yours. Got us both done in one day." Arthur sets a can in front of me, cracks it open, and flashes me a smile. Without wasting another second, I tip it back and take a large drink. My eyes start to water from the bubbles, and the taste makes my face scrunch up. Mr. Murphy chuckles. "Not much of a drinker, huh?"

I shake my head. "Nope. It might taste like shit, but somehow it still feels good going down." I won't tell him it's because the bruise permanently on my heart has been poked.

He takes a swig from his dark beer bottle and grins. "You're so much like her."

I don't even need to ask who he's talking about. I'm well aware of the impact my grandmother had on me. But sometimes, I forget what she meant to this town. What she meant to Mr. Murphy. She always said they were soul mates fighting to get to each other and both kept missing the bus.

I take another drink. "No I'm not. She was on an entirely different level. I could only dream of being half the woman she was."

"Oh dear, you need to look a little closer. You are everything she was and are far more than you give yourself credit for."

I tighten my chin, pulling my bottom lip up so it doesn't quiver. "That's really nice of you to say. Thank you."

"I miss her," he whispers before downing the remainder of liquid in his bottle.

"Me too." He stands, pats my shoulder, and walks away.

I gulp down the rest of the skinny can and hiccup as I set it back on the bar. "Arthur," I call out since the three other guys from the fire department who are working the bar are down at the other end, chatting with none other than Zeena. Mason's right. She keeps popping up all over the place. I spotted her at the grocery store yesterday when I was there too. The nasty looks she gives me make me laugh. Which just pisses her off even more. I probably shouldn't get as much enjoyment out of it as I do.

"Another one, please," I shout, and Arthur keeps them coming.

I'm not like her. She was strong and fearless. I seem to be afraid of everything and fake my strength every day. Truth is, the more I try to get my life just the way I want it, the further from it I feel.

Soon, I've got four empty cans in front of me. I forgot what it feels like to be really buzzed from alcohol. I push away from the bar and take a few uneasy steps.

"Whoa. You gonna be all right there, Andi?" Arthur asks.

"I'm good. Heading home."

"You want me to walk you? They can handle the beer tent without me for a few minutes."

"Nope. I can make it." I stumble on a divot in the grass but catch myself before I fall.

"You sure? You look a little…"

"I'm fine, Arthur. I know where my house is."

Not wanting to draw attention to myself, I walk behind all of the tents and across the grass. The ground starts to tilt the closer I get to the cement bathroom building. I hold on to the side of it and blink, trying to rid my eyes of the distortion.

"Are you okay?" I feel a hand around my waist, and I pick my head up, but the face in front of me is not the one I want to see.

"Hey, Bobby. I'm good. Just a few drinks."

I lean my shoulder into the building, and the strap from my black tank top falls off my shoulder. His eyes move over my body and to my lips. He pushes a piece of my hair behind my ear, and I don't like it. I pull away, but he moves in closer and drags his hand down my shoulder until he has the strap of my shirt in his fingertips. He tugs it down.

"Stop it, Bobby."

"C'mon, I'll take you home."

He pulls me from the wall, and I fight him. "I don't want you to take me home. I can get home all by myself."

"It's been a long time, Andrea. A long time I've waited. For you."

"What the hell are you talking about?" He puts his hand on my hip and digs his fingertips into my skin. I smack his hand away. "Stop fucking touching me."

"Every summer, I would come to my aunt's just because I knew you would be in town. You had to know. I was here for you. I'm here for you now."

I push myself off the wall, trying to get away from him. "I'm sorry. Not interested." He pulls my arm, spins me around, and kisses me. "I said no," I yell and push him. But I lose my footing and fall backward. Strong arms catch me and gently guide me down to the grass. My vision blurs as the world starts tilting, and two large shadows step over me. I hear yelling and a scuffle, so I try to stand up again, but my legs are too shaky, and I fall into the wall headfirst. I touch my hand to my head and throw up all over the ground.

———

I SUCK in a harsh breath as ice touches my forehead. "What the hell?" I mumble. Fighting the pain in my eyes, I blink until the world around me comes clear. Mason is sitting on my coffee table, leaning over me and holding a kitchen towel filled with ice. I try to sit up but only make it an inch off the couch before my head throbs harder.

"Don't get up." He grabs a glass of water with a straw and holds it up as I take a few sips.

"Oh my God. What happened to your hand?" Mason's knuckles are usually a little beat up from work, but they look busted open.

"Someone forgot their fucking manners. He remembers them now."

Images of Bobby putting his hands on me flash in my head.

"Where's Bobby?"

"He's gone."

"What do you mean gone?" I ask, still feeling the swirling in my head. "Gone like he went home or gone like there's a mysterious pile of dirt somewhere?"

He chuckles. "Tucker and a few other guys managed to pull Lucas and me off of the fucker before we killed him."

"Mason?"

"Yeah?"

"I think I'm going to throw up."

He grabs me from the couch and hustles through the living room to the bathroom. He sets me down in front of the toilet and holds my hair as the rest of tonight's mistake removes itself from my body.

"This is why I don't drink," I say, wiping my mouth, flushing the toilet, and propping myself up on the floor against the tub.

"You drank at Tana and Lucas's wedding though. You seemed fine."

I slowly move my eyes around the bathroom until they meet his. He's on the floor too, leaning up against the wall. "Fine. I don't drink when I'm upset."

"Why are you upset?"

He's really asking me this. If I was of clear mind, I would keep my mouth shut. Besides, I'm not innocent in this. I agreed that friends is as far as we go. But I'm not of clear mind, and my mouth is full of the truth.

"Because of you." I pull myself from the floor, and Mason jumps up. My body feels wobbly as I stand at the sink and grab my mouthwash. I do a quick swish and spit and turn toward Mason. "The light in here is killing my head."

"Back to the living room?"

I want to go to bed. But that's the worst place I can have Mason take me. I'll want him to wrap me up in his warm arms and feel his breath against my skin as he sleeps. "Yep. Couch." He wraps his arm around my waist and steadies my steps to the couch. He lays me down, takes his place on the coffee table again, and puts the ice back on my head.

"Is it bad?" I ask him.

"You should see him."

"Oh my God. I'm going to hear from his aunt tomorrow, I just know it."

"Then you can give her my phone number, and I'll tell her what a piece of shit her nephew is and that if I see him near you again, it will take a lot more than a few people in town to pull me off him."

"Mason, he barely…"

"He. Touched. You. The end."

"I had it under control," I stammer.

"Sober Andi would have kicked his ass. Drunk Andi couldn't even stop herself from falling into the wall."

I press my hand against the scrape on my pounding head and wince. "Yeah, my head hurts."

He chuckles. "This couch is dumb. Let's get you settled in bed."

Before I can protest, Mason scoops me up in his arms and carries me to my bedroom. He sits me on the edge of the bed, picks up the folded gray silk nightgown from my pillow, and sets it in my lap. His fingers grip the bottom hem of my shirt and lift it over my head.

"Hey, you getting a peeksy?"

He smiles. "A peeksy? No. I'm getting you dressed and in bed."

I reach around and unfasten my bra, letting it fall down my arms and to the floor. I can hear him whisper, "Jesus," as he quickly puts the nightgown over my head.

"Lay back, let me get these jeans off."

The spinning has started to fade, and I'm thankful for that as I lie back and feel the jeans slide down my legs. His warm hands grab my ankles as he turns my body, tucks my legs under the covers, and pulls them up to my chin.

"You hit your head, so I'm not leaving. I'll be in the living room if you need me for anything."

"Mason?"

"Yeah."

"Lay with me."

He hangs his head for a second before pulling his wallet and phone from his pocket, setting them on the nightstand, and crawling in next to me. Facing each other, I study his tight, rigid jaw.

"Why did you say that I should listen to Zeena?"

"Because I hurt people."

"I don't think you'd hurt me."

"I never want to hurt you."

"Then why do you keep pulling away from me."

He takes a deep breath, and I reach out to caress that tick in his jaw away. He grips my hand, kisses my palm, and aims his hazel eyes at me. "My mother left when I was nine. Just left. She broke my father's heart into a million pieces." He swallows and looks at my hand. "She shattered mine. How can a person be such a good mother one day and the next just lose all interest and leave? She never called, never texted, never wrote. My father and I never saw her again. Dad found out she had met a guy at work, and she left us for him. I had a real hard time trusting people after that."

A dull ache settles in my chest as I listen to the pain in his voice. "Who could blame you? I understand."

He shakes his head. "It gets worse."

Worse? I'm afraid to hear any more. But Mason is talking, and I'm going to listen.

"I had a hard time committing to anyone. Never staying too long. Never giving them the chance to hurt me. Until Arianna."

Fuck. I hope I don't regret listening to this. "Who's Arianna?"

"She was the first woman I ever trusted with my heart. I was with her for a few years, and we got engaged."

"Engaged," I blurt, a little too loud.

"I came home early from work and found her in our bed fucking another man."

An ache I've worked hard to rid myself of weighs heavy in my chest. He's been through hell. One I know a little too much about. "I'm so sorry."

"I can still see the diamond on her hand sparkle in the light as it rested on his back."

"That had to be awful. What did you do?"

"I ended up in prison."

I sit up fast and grab my head and my stomach. "Did you kill him?"

He laughs and gently pulls me back down to the pillow. "Almost. I ripped him off of her and kicked his naked ass. Then I took his car out for a joyride before I drove into the lake. Ending of that story is I was charged with battery and grand larceny, and I never trusted another woman again."

"What about Zeena?"

"I trust Zeena about as much as someone who claims the sky is purple. In the beginning I tried, but I couldn't make myself care about what she was doing, where she was at, or who she was with. And when she threatened to leave, I shrugged and told her goodbye. I didn't care at all. I'm not proud of how I made her feel. But I couldn't make myself love her."

"I get it. That's why you wanted to be friends. Because you can't make yourself care about me in that way either."

I swallow the lump in my throat and try to keep my sour belly calm. My eyes feel about as heavy as my head does.

"No. I care about you so much it hurts when you're away. I want to be with you. I want you to be mine. And it scares the hell out of me."

Darkness starts to take over as the weight of the evening mixed with the alcohol makes it impossible to stay awake.

"I was yours the second you put your lips against mine," I whisper and feel his gentle kiss on my forehead as I pass out.

CHAPTER NINE

MASON

"Do you need a bib?" Lucas asks. "You're dribbling soup down your chin. Iris eats better than you."

"Shit," I say, wiping my mouth.

"If you could peel your eyes away from Andi for two seconds, you could probably avoid having to change your shirt before we go back to work."

"Shut up." I chuckle and wipe the drops that fell onto the table.

Lucas and I have come into the diner for lunch every day this past week. I can't see her enough. Even after spending every evening together, I'm still anxious to see her the next day. Last Saturday when I brought her home from Fall Fest, everything changed for me. I've never felt the way I felt watching Andi sleep that night. The wall of denial crumbled when she said she was mine. I had been fighting my feelings for some time.

"Just don't do anything stupid," Lucas says.

"What the hell does that mean?"

"Tana told me last night that Andi finally opened up to her about her ex."

"Her ex? It's not like I assumed she hadn't dated before, but I've been around this town for a while now, and I've never heard about an ex of hers."

"None of us did. I guess it was a long time ago, but according to Tana, he was scum. Treated Andi like shit, and I guess he cheated on her and then just left her somewhere. I don't know, I could tell Tana wasn't giving me all the details, but it's really none of my business."

My spoon hits the side of my bowl. I've lost my appetite.

Fuck. "That's why she had such a knowing look in her eye when I told her about Arianna." She knows what that feels like.

"Who's Arianna?"

My eyes shoot to Lucas, realizing that I said it out loud.

"You know how I ended up in prison? Kicking that guy's ass, stealing his car, and driving it into the lake?"

"Yeah," Lucas says, his eyebrows drawn together.

"I caught him fucking my fiancée."

I wait for Lucas to call me a dumbass for throwing so many years of my life away on something stupid. But he doesn't even flinch.

"It all makes so much sense now. Why wouldn't you have told me?"

"It's embarrassing. Such a stupid mistake over someone who didn't even give a shit about me."

"You should know me better than that, brother. You loved her, and we can do some pretty stupid shit when love is involved."

"It feels even more stupid now."

"Why is that?"

"I don't know if I even knew what love was back then." Andi

runs out of the kitchen, and her eyes hit mine with a gleam before she disappears into her office.

Lucas's grin spreads across his face. "Because you definitely know what it feels like now. Don't you?"

Yeah. I think I do.

"ARE you sure you'll be okay?"

Andi rolls her eyes at the same question I've asked her fifteen times. "Yes, Mason. I'm going to be fine. Go enjoy your best friend's bachelor party."

I would rather shove rusty nails into my eye than leave her right now. They still haven't figured out who threw the rock through the diner window, and I haven't figured out who left that note on the back door. I haven't forgotten about her eerie feelings of someone watching her, but with Andi's permission, Owen's been trying to keep an eye on the video cameras outside of her house as much as he can. He hasn't seen anything unusual in the footage.

"Tucker is aware I'm leaving and will be ready if you need him for anything. He's going to make a few extra patrols around your house and the diner. You have his number programmed into your phone, right?"

"Yes, Mason," she says, annoyed. "I'm going to be fine."

"I wish you were coming with me. You still sure you can't swing it with the diner?"

"Oh yeah, that would be great. I'll tag along on Everest's bachelor party. I'm not knocking women who do, but I don't really get off on seeing boobs."

"Boobs? What the hell are you talking about?"

"Don't men usually go to a strip club or something for bachelor parties?"

She's trying to hide it, but I can see a little bit of apprehension in her eyes. I sit down next to her, place my finger under her chin, and turn her head so she looks at me.

"We aren't built that way. Once we're taken, we're taken. My brothers and I don't want another woman in our face. We want our women in our face."

Her lips part as her eyes search mine. "Are you taken, Mason?"

I nod. "So are you. And I would never do anything to jeopardize that."

She smiles sweetly as relief takes over her face. I know she needed to hear that.

"Neither would I," she whispers, knowing I need to hear it from her too.

I press my lips to hers, and she inhales sharply through her nose. I don't want the kiss to end, but my phone chirps in my pocket.

"Damn, I don't want to go."

"Yes you do. You'll have such a great time. It's only a few days."

She hugs me tightly as I wrap my arms around her. *Please, God, keep her safe while I'm gone.* "I'll call you later tonight."

I kiss her again, touch her cheek, and walk out of the house.

———

Looking around the table at the men who've become family, I can't say that I regret losing my shit all those years ago. Prison was a hellhole, and every day I was just trying to survive. But if I didn't go there, I wouldn't be here.

"I am too old to drink like that," Everest says, sitting across from me at Owen's patio table.

"Here," Paul, one of Everest's best friends, says, tossing him a bottle of aspirin. Paul was in prison with Everest, Owen, and Lucas, but I didn't know him until the boys introduced me. Everest seems to have a special bond with everyone for different reasons. He's the foundation of the circle. I'm just so damn lucky they brought me into it.

Owen and Natalie's baby starts to fuss as Lucas readjusts her on his chest.

"Please don't start crying now, sweet pea," Owen says across the table to his baby girl. "My head can't take it."

I think we all drank a little too much down at the fire last night. Not only does Andi not have to worry about me gallivanting the countryside, these men are not about that life either. All Everest wanted for his bachelor party was all of us together and drinks by the fire at Owen's lodge. I don't think I've laughed so hard in my life.

Natalie, Owen's wife, steps out onto the patio, holding a plate of bacon. She moves the boxes of donuts that Lucas went and picked up this morning and sets the plate in front of him.

"I'm scared," he says, patting Starling's bum.

"I perfected it. Try one."

Lucas grabs one from the plate and shoves it into his mouth. His eyes widen before he pretends to wipe a tear. "I've never been prouder in my entire life. Congratulations. You finally did it." He turns to the baby in his arms and says, "You're safe now. You can thank Uncle Lucas for all your future breakfasts later."

The table erupts in laughter. "I can finally sleep at night knowing my bacon is up to your standards, Whack. Now give me my baby," she teases.

I still get caught off guard sometimes when they use the nicknames they had in prison. Everest didn't have a nickname, but it could be because he's as tall and big as Mount Everest, so his name fits him. Nobody messed with Everest. But Owen was known as Gill, and Lucas was known as Whack. The nicknames have slowly begun to fade, but every once in a while, one gets used, and it reminds me all over again of how far we've all come.

Lucas pulls away. "I'm not done holding her yet."

"Do you have boobs?" Natalie asks.

"If he keeps eating sprinkle donuts and bacon the way he does, I'm sure he will soon," Owen says.

"I have to feed her. You're here until tomorrow. You'll have plenty of time to hold her."

He snarls, kisses her cheek, and hands her over to Natalie. She snuggles Starling and walks back inside as Lucas grabs the last sprinkle donut and puts a piece of bacon on top before he takes a big bite.

"You are just an overgrown man child. How Tana puts up with you, I'll never know," Owen says.

"I don't think any of us can explain how our women put up with us," Paul says.

"Speaking of," I say, and all the men turn to look at me. "We got any plans today?"

Lucas grins. "Why? Anxious to get home to someone in particular?"

"Yeah," I say, and instead of laughing at Lucas's attempt at a joke, they all nod approvingly.

"You know I'm here if you need anything from me," Owen says.

"I appreciate that, brother."

"Any idea who could be behind the weird shit going on?" Everest asks.

"My best guess is maybe some kids being stupid. We just had homecoming, and they toilet papered damn near every house in town. But I hate how it feels being this far away."

"I'm just hanging out until a little later this afternoon," Everest says. "If you want to take off early and head home, that's cool with me. I'm just glad you got down here for a few nights."

"I woke up to a leak in the kitchen this morning. I've got to get that taken care of before I leave," Lucas says and turns to Paul. "You can drop me off on your way back to Boston, can't you?"

"For sure," Paul says.

"We've all been there, brother. If it feels like you need to get back home to her, then you should go," Owen says. "Trust your gut. When it comes to our women, always trust your gut."

"Absolutely," Everest says. "Now get the hell out of here. We'll see you next week for the wedding, and you better be bringing her with you."

———

WHEN I TALKED to Andi yesterday, I told her it would be midnight before I got back into town, but the sun has just set. We made plans for tomorrow, but I can't wait to see her. I can almost feel her in the palm of my hand, and my body is full of adrenaline as I turn down her street. That adrenaline escalates but for the wrong reasons as I look at an SUV I've never seen before in Andi's driveway. I park in front of the house next door and walk slowly up to Andi's window to look inside. I will kill anyone who dares try to hurt her. But as the room comes into view, no one is trying to hurt Andi.

Her back is to me, and I can't see her face, but her hair is wrapped up in a towel. Someone's hands travel down her back until they rest on her ass. She isn't struggling. Someone isn't attacking her. This man is kissing her, and from the looks of it, she's kissing him back. My throat feels like it's closing. I can't feel the ground beneath my feet. Just like before, it feels like I'm floating above myself, unable to land on solid ground. I want to march in there and tear his tongue out. But it didn't make me feel better before, and it isn't going to make me feel better now. As a tear slides down my cheek, I run back to my car, get in, and drive away from Andi.

CHAPTER TEN

Andi

MASON DIDN'T CALL me last night, but I assumed he wouldn't since he was getting in so late. I bet getting up this morning for work wasn't too delightful for him either. It's weird going to the grocery store in the middle of the day on a Monday. But because my parents are in town, I want to make a nice dinner. I'm a little nervous about how Mason might take me asking him to meet and have dinner with my family tonight. I'll ease him into the idea, but I don't want to push him too fast.

"Are you going to tell me what you're making tonight, or am I going to have to guess from the ingredients on this list?" Dad asks.

"Tuscan chicken with a creamy gnocchi soup."

"My favorite," he says, rubbing his belly. "I miss you being so close."

"Me too." I love my parents, but my dad and I have a special relationship. Mama and I have always butted heads about things, and Dad, he's always been my backup. Always sticking up for me and making it up to her later. They have one hell of a relationship though. Like two horny teenagers, they can barely keep their hands off each other. It's really disgusting.

Dad and I head into the little market on the edge of town. They don't have everything that a normal big-chain grocery store has, but I know they have what I need for dinner tonight. Otherwise, we would have had to take a trip to Birkenshire.

"I'm going to see if they have your mama's nail polish remover she requested."

"Aisle five," I tell him. "I'll be in the produce section."

He heads off in one direction, and I go to find the spinach. My body quakes with excitement when Mason comes into view as I come around the aisle. I feel a little pathetic for how much I missed him just for these few days.

"Hey, sexy," I say, walking up behind him. He spins around, but his face isn't full of excitement or happiness. He looks drained and really pissed off.

"Did you enjoy last night?" he asks, a disgusted look on his face.

"What are you talking about?"

"I trusted you. Gave you something I didn't think I would be able to give anyone ever again. But I put my heart in your hand, and you squeezed the last bit of life out of it."

"Hold up," I say, frantic. "You can trust me. I'm so confused. What happened?"

"I saw you. I came home early and saw a car in your driveway. I peeked through the window and saw you standing in the living room, kissing a man with dark hair. How fucking could you?"

"What? I absolutely was not kissing anyone. Are you sure you didn't see my…"

"Hey," Dad says, walking up. "I think you better lower your tone and watch your mouth when you're talking to her."

Mason throws the head of lettuce he was holding to the ground and stares at my dad with that scary look in his eye.

"Mason, calm down." I press my hand to his chest and push on him, as if I had even the smallest chance of moving him. "Dad, I can handle this."

Mason's head flies in my direction. "Dad?"

"Yes, Mason…meet my dad, Henry. Dad, this is…Mason. This is not how I saw the two of you meeting."

The color drains from Mason's face as he runs his hand over his hair. "I saw you kissing someone through the window, and your hair was wrapped up in a towel," he says, moving his eyes from me to Dad. "Your hair… It was you. But, I saw you kissing someone."

"Yes, you did," Dad says. "My wife."

I should be offended by Mason's lack of trust in our new relationship. But knowing what he's been through, and what he thought he saw, I just can't blame him.

"Wait until you see my mama, Mason," I say, unable to control the laugh that builds in my chest. "People say we look like sisters all the time. Except she has platinum-blonde hair."

"Which was wrapped up in a towel," Dad says, also finding the situation a little amusing. "I can see how that may have looked from your perspective."

"I'm sorry," Mason says to Dad. He grabs my hand, relief flooding every one of his features. "I'm so sorry, babe."

"It's okay. I'm just glad we got it straightened out." He pulls me in and wraps me up in his large warm arms. He kisses my neck, and chills run through me.

"I fucking missed the hell out of you," he whispers. "I should've known better. You would never."

"You're right. I would *never*."

"Mason," Dad says as Mason loosens his grip on me. "Starting over. I'm Henry. Nice to meet you."

"Good to meet you too, sir," Mason says, reaching his hand out to shake Dad's.

"You can drop the sir. It's just Henry. I can tell the two of you need a minute. I'll just go grab a few more things on the list." He shakes the list in his hand, nods, and walks away.

Mason grips my hips, and I can feel the desperation in them. "I feel like such an asshole."

"You're not an asshole. You were hurt, and I understand that. I know how you can make it up to me, but I don't want you to do something you aren't ready for."

He nuzzles my neck and kisses my skin. "Name it."

"Will you have dinner with my parents tonight? They aren't in town very often, and I'd love for them to get to know you."

"What time am I coming?" he asks, peppering more kisses along my jaw.

"That's it? You're just agreeing to come?"

He breathes me in as his lips finally make it to mine. He presses hard, and his fingers flex against my skin.

"I'll do just about anything for you, Andi. If you want me to have dinner with your parents, then I'll have dinner with your parents."

"Six thirty," I say, kissing him back and wishing we were alone. Even better in my office on the desk that I'll never look at the same again.

"Can I bring anything?"

"Just you."

"Where the hell does this place keep sun-dried tomatoes?" Dad says from one aisle over, and I laugh.

"I better go. I'll see you tonight?"

"You'll see me every night you want me."

I smile. "Every night it is."

He gives me one more chaste kiss and takes his hands from my body, leaving it cold and yearning for him. With a palpitating heart and the heat smoldering inside, I take a deep breath and focus on dinner. And helping my dad find the rest of what we need.

———

"EVERYTHING SMELLS SO GOOD, SWEETHEART." Mama blows on her fresh red nail polish as she sits at the table in the dine-in kitchen. My grandmother always told me this was her favorite room. It was mine too when she was here. If I wasn't helping her, I would sit at that table and watch her cook as she told me stories of her life. I can almost feel her in this kitchen with me and Mama.

"Mama, I need to tell you something, but I need you to keep an open mind."

"Oh dear Jesus. You're trying to kill me tonight, aren't you? New boyfriend, shocking news—are you poisoning the soup as well?"

"Okay, Drama Mama. Take a breath." She takes a deep breath as I stir the soup and then join her at the table. "I want to tell you because I don't want you to find out by accident and get surprised by it."

"Just spill it, Andrea. You have no idea what kind of circumstances my mind is creating right now. Out with it."

"Mason was in prison." Mama busts out laughing, but eventually she sees my straight face, and her expression drops. "Please, just let me explain. His mother left him and his dad when he was young and never came back. He had a hard time trusting people. Women in particular. After years, he finally let himself fall in love, and he was going to marry her. Only he walked into their home and found her in their bed with another man."

Mama might be a little too pretentious, but she has the best heart. I need her to understand that Mason is a good guy. "That's awful. But how did he end up in prison?"

"He beat the guy up, stole his expensive car, and drove it into a lake. He was crushed already, and she pulverized him."

Mama's eyes glaze over. "I don't know how I feel about this." She places her hand on her cheek and stills for a moment before her face softens and she looks back at me. "And...you love him. Don't you?"

Like a brisk wind just hit my sails, I smile. I have been refusing to allow myself to accept this up until now. "Yeah, Mama. I love him."

Mama knows the fresh hell of heartbreak I went through. She's been telling me for years to "find a nice boy" and settle down. Plant roots. Tears well up in her eyes as joy fills her. But it only lasts for a moment before they get wide.

"Oh my God." She moves her hand from her chest to her mouth. "What is Daddy gonna say?"

"I already told him. We were worried about you," I say, laughing.

"Me?" she shrieks.

"Yeah. We never know how Drama Mama is going to react."

A knock comes from the front door, and Mama's concern turns to excitement. We jump up from the table and walk through the living room, and I open the door. Mason smiles, and Mama grips my arm as she looks over my shoulder. He's in a black collared shirt and dark jeans and has two bouquets of flowers in his hands. If my parents weren't here, dinner would be burning, and Mason would be in my bed.

"Hi," I say, holding in the "fuck me" I really want to say.

"Hey," he says, his eyes hitting mine. He hands me one of the bouquets, and Mama steps out from behind me.

"I'm Joann. Pleasure to meet you," Mama says.

"These are for you." He hands Mama the other bouquet. "It's nice to meet you too."

Mama takes the flowers and gasps. "What a gentleman. You didn't have to do that." She pushes up on her toes and gives him a hug. Seeing her pull him in touches my heart.

I have a feeling Mama just fell in love with Mason too. I giggle as she runs to Daddy, who just walked in the back door from outside. "Look what Mason brought. Flowers for Andrea and me."

"That's a good man," he says, walking past her, through the kitchen, and up to us. He puts his hand out to shake Mason's. "Glad you could make it."

Daddy releases Mason's hand and walks back into the kitchen with Mama.

"I'm glad you came too," I say, pressing up on my toes and kissing him. He moans softly into my mouth. "Don't make that sound. I'm two seconds away from ditching these people and taking you back to your place."

An evil grin comes across his face. "One more word and I will lose all the manners my father gave me, Andi."

I laugh and back down. "My parents leave tomorrow."

"Then tomorrow night, you're mine."

My phone rings from the kitchen. "Here you go, dear," Mama says, jogging to me with my phone.

The number isn't one I recognize, but I pick it up anyway. "Hello?" The only noise from the other end is slow, shallow breathing. "Hello?" Mason's eyebrows furrow as he touches my arm. I cover the microphone with my hand. "They're not answering, but I can tell someone is there," I whisper to Mason. He holds his hand out, and I give him the phone.

"You have two seconds to answer," he says sternly into the phone. Then he hangs up the call.

"Everything all right?" Daddy asks, walking into the room.

"Of course," Mason says.

"Good because you should probably do something about that soup," Daddy says to me. "It looks like it's boiling over." Daddy laughs as he walks down the hallway to the room they're staying in.

"Shit," I say, jogging toward the kitchen, following Mama. I stop just before the kitchen and turn around to Mason. "Everything is okay, right?"

"Yeah. I'm sure it was just a telemarketer. They do that all the time," Mason says and winks at me.

I smile and turn around into the kitchen. Mama shut the stove burner off, so I pop my head back into the living room. But Mason isn't in there. He's outside the picture window, talking on his cell phone as he looks at my cell phone. I didn't think Mason thought that phone call was a telemarketer any more than I did.

CHAPTER ELEVEN

MASON

OTHER THAN WITH THE GUYS, I haven't sat down to a family dinner in years. My dad had a hard time with me going to prison, and even though we still talk from time to time, the relationship we had just faded away. He was so disappointed in me. I was disappointed in myself. But I wasn't prepared for how strained just sitting next to him would be once I got out. It was awkward and uncomfortable for both of us. So it's weird sitting here with Andi's dad, having a drink and feeling nothing but at ease.

Henry pats his belly. "I'm glad I don't live around here all the time. I would weigh two tons. How the hell do you do it?"

I laugh. "I work out, and I'm pretty sure I lose enough weight in sweat on a hot summer day on a roof."

He chuckles and takes a casual swig of his scotch. "Jokes aside. You wanna tell me about that phone call Andi got today? Didn't like your expression when you got on the line."

Henry is a straight shooter, and it's probably the reason we are getting along so well. No sugarcoating, no beating around the bush. He's observant and doesn't hesitate to ask questions.

"How much has Andi told you about what's been going on around here?"

"The front was open, she found a key, the rock in her window at the diner, and she said she felt like she was being watched a few times, but she's managed to convince herself it's just the neighbors being nosey."

"Yep. I also found a sticky note on the back door of the diner. I didn't tell Andi about that because I was handling things like placing cameras at the diner and here at the house." I point to the few I set up around the back of the house.

"What did the note say?"

"'I hate you.' I talked to the cook, and he said his ex-wife messes with him sometimes. He said she definitely hates him, so the note was just too broad to nail down who it was for. I'll admit, I was starting to think it was all just terrible coincidences."

"But you didn't like that phone call."

I shake my head. "I'm taking care of it. I have a friend that…" I hesitate to tell him about how Owen can get any kind of information I want. I called Owen the second Andi walked out of the room and gave him the phone number. I'm just waiting for him to get back home to his computer so he can investigate it.

"Just tell me. I already know more about you than you think. Andi told me everything."

"You know I was in prison, then?" I get a text from Owen that sets my soul on fire. I shoot Owen a quick text back, asking him to see where the phone is located, and try to keep my focus on the conversation with Henry.

"I do. I don't like that. But I'm not going to judge you about what you did in your past. But you can bet I'm going to judge the shit out of the way you treat my daughter."

"I'll bury myself to protect her."

"I had a feeling you would say that. Watching the two of you at dinner and hearing you say that is all the proof I need. Now, what do you know about that call?"

I glance at the new text from Owen. He thinks the phone was destroyed because he can't find the location. I shake my head, remembering Andi's dad sitting next to me. Tucker needs to know about this phone call. I'm keeping him in on every detail, no matter how small. I send Tucker a quick text to fill him in.

"Sorry," I apologize for being on my phone, and he waves me off. "It was a burner phone. Used once and we think ditched."

"Could it have been a wrong number?" he asks, scratching his chin.

"Possible. Nothing is adding up."

"Maybe we should cancel our trip," Henry says. "I don't know how I'll be able to leave knowing she's in trouble."

"I can't make that decision for you. That's between you guys and Andi. There's a lot of weird coincidences happening, but I don't know what's going on. Lucas, Tucker, and I are watching things as closely as we can, and so far, we haven't been able to put together anything that makes sense. Make no mistake, I'm not dropping my guard at all. I have a wedding to go to next week in Tennessee, and I was going to ask her anyway, but now I don't think I can go if she won't come with me. I'm not comfortable with leaving her here alone either."

"Good luck. She hates weddings."

His statement takes me aback. I didn't know this about her. "She went to Lucas and Tana's wedding."

"When she cares about someone, she'll put herself through hell to make them happy. Tana is her best friend. She wasn't going to miss that and make Tana upset."

"Why does she hate weddings?"

"I see she hasn't told you. It doesn't surprise me." Henry takes another drink from his rocks glass. "I'm only telling you this because I think you deserve to know, and I don't think she'll ever tell you. Andi had a wedding. Two hundred and fifty people were there." My heart sinks. I'm not sure I want to hear this. "She looked so beautiful in a big sparkly white dress. She planned every detail of the wedding herself. She was so excited to see me when I walked into the bridal suite. I would've given anything not to have to tell her the groom wasn't coming and there would be no wedding. I've never seen someone go from euphoric to completely broken within seconds. And he did. He fucking broke my girl. She shut down and didn't talk to anyone for a long time. Except for my mother. She came down here and spent months in this house, trying to rebuild what he broke. I don't think I've seen all her pieces back together again. Until tonight. You make her happy, and I'm grateful. But if she breaks again, I'll be the one in prison."

———

I FIX my tie and the top button of my tuxedo shirt in a tiny mirror on the other side of one of the kitchen cabinets in my camper. "Andi. We're going to be late," I shout. Andi tried to make the excuse that she didn't want to leave the diner, but I assured her that Jessica seems capable of taking care of the place when she needs to. I didn't tell her what her father told me. I'm glad I know, but I'm not about to bring that up to her and dig up those memories. Tana talked her into coming, and I owe her big-time.

I see movement in the corner of the mirror when Andi steps into view. I spin around, and my heart beats harder than ever before. Andi's dark hair is curled and loosely pulled up on top of her head, showing off dangling gold earrings. Her smooth skin is adorned with an emerald-green satin dress that hugs the curve of her hips and stops just below her knee, though a slit on only her left side teases me with glimpses of her leg. The top cuts across her full breasts, showing just enough cleavage to make me nuts. "Wow." I lick my lip, hoping to stop myself from drooling. "You look fucking incredible."

"You haven't seen the best part."

"Babe, I can't imagine anything could get better than this." She slowly spins, and my knees feel weak. "Fuck me," I whisper, grabbing my chest. The only thing on her back is straps crisscrossing from one side to the other over her bare skin into a V-shape stopping at her lower back. I move to her and breathe heavily as I take her in my arms. "God, I want you right now." I kiss her neck and press my body into hers.

"Mason, behave," she giggles. "We have to go."

"We're not going." This time, her laugh radiates through me.

"When this wedding is over, you can rip the damn thing off me. But right now, we have to go."

I growl and pull myself away from her. This day is going to last forever. I walk Andi to the grassy area of the lodge, where all the chairs are set up. The lodge has become home and a meeting place for all of us. Owen got married here, and so did Lucas. It only makes sense that Everest does too.

"Are you sure you're going to be okay?" I hate that Andi has to sit by herself during the wedding since I'm standing up for Everest.

"I swear, I'm fine. I'd tell you if I wasn't. Now go." She shoos me away, and I kiss her before running all the way up the hill to Owen's house, where the guys are waiting to walk down together.

———

I LOCK eyes with Andi the second I take my place next to the guys at the altar. There's a hint of pain in her eyes as she watches Danielle walk down the aisle. As the wedding progresses, I notice her wipe a few tears as she smiles. And when they walk down the aisle as husband and wife, she cheers and cries again. After the talk with Henry, I assumed Andi never wanted to get married, and if I'm being honest with myself, it was kind of a relief. But as I watch her, I'm not sure if that's true.

The reception is held in a big white tent across the grassy field from the altar. Watching Everest marry the love of his life makes me realize that there's a soul mate for everyone. Even Everest. He always told us he'd never let someone in again. But we knew his heart was too good to be wasted. He just had to find Dani.

After the food, toasts, and a few hours of dancing, I'm ready to go. I find Andi laughing with Tana at a round table with a glass of champagne in her hand. "Are you ready?" I ask her.

"Don't you think it's too early for you to leave?" Tana asks Mason, teasing him. She doesn't know Lucas walked up behind her at the same time.

"You've worn that dress for too long, woman," Lucas says to Tana. "Let's go take care of that."

Tana smirks at Andi and fake yawns. "Just kidding. I'm so tired," she says and gives Andi a wink. "I'll see you tomorrow." Tana jumps up from her seat, and Lucas takes her hand and rushes her out of the tent.

Andi laughs and sets her glass down. "I'm ready."

I hold my hand out to her, and she takes it, pulling herself out of her seat. I lightly push her to walk in front of me so I can watch her hips as she alternates steps down the path. The entire walk to my camper, I fight the carnal urge to take her right here. My palms sweat, and my heart beats faster as she lifts her dress, revealing even more of her perfect shape to move up the steps to the door. Reaching around her, I pull on the handle and push it open for her. She sighs as she kicks off her shoes, but the second the door latches behind me, I'm on her.

All night, I've wanted to hold her in my arms. Tell her I'd never hurt her like he did. Erase all that pain and turn it into something beautiful. I'm going to show her that I can love her more than anyone else ever has. That I want her and no one else ever again. I grab her wrist and pull her back to me, spinning her just before her body hits mine. I sink my hands deep into her hair and kiss her like I haven't been able to kiss her before. She clutches my arms tightly as she swirls her tongue with mine, matching the intensity that I feel surging through me. The dimmed overhead light throughout the camper highlights her collarbones, and I traipse my fingers over each one. Our kiss softens as I drag my fingers down her back. She breaks from our lips and tilts her head back. The sparkle in her eye mesmerizes me. Puts me in some kind of trance where my mouth doesn't hear the part of my brain telling me not to say it.

"I think I'm falling in love with you." Her closed lips tip up at the sides as the sparkle from the dim light starts to blur from the water gathering at her lash line. "I lied," I blurt. "I'm not falling. I've landed, Andi. I'm so fucking in love with you."

She presses her fingertips harder into the fabric of my button-up dress shirt. For a moment, I wish I hadn't said it. Her eyes search mine, and the moment of silence makes my stomach drop. Did I just scare away the only woman I've ever truly loved?

CHAPTER TWELVE

Andi

HEARING those words from Mason takes my breath away. I never thought I wanted to hear them again. I've been so afraid that I wouldn't be able to believe them. Words can be just that. The formation of the tongue and lips to create sound. But it's so different coming from Mason. I could *feel* every letter and sound straight into my soul.

"I love you too," I whisper, finally finding my ability to speak. The elation that spreads across his face is all it takes to melt away years of anguish, making everything I've gone through worth it. Every tear, every broken beat of my heart, every sad, tormented day. I'd do it all again if it meant I get this moment with him.

He plants a powerful kiss on my lips, taking me. His fingertips traipse over the straps on my back gently, but his rugged working hands aren't so gentle when they land on the curves of my ass. He hauls me up, and I wrap my legs around his waist as his tongue delightfully assaults mine. I'm jostled as he kicks off his shoes without ever taking his lips from mine, and then he moves back to the bedroom as I run my hands feverishly over his head, pulling his kiss harder into mine. The need to feel his skin on mine, his taste on my tongue, his love inside of me is so strong, I can't breathe. Unable to loosen my hold on him, he lays us both down on the soft mattress, putting one arm to the side to support his weight.

The faint music from the reception mixes with the sound of our kiss and heavy breaths. My dress falls at the slit, and his hand finds my knee and runs down my leg and up my dress. I whimper into his mouth as he grips my ass and pulls my core into his erection. He easily slides against my satin gown, sending my nerve endings into a tizzy but only making the desire for him more intense. I reach between us, work his belt, button, and zipper open, but I can't push his pants down enough to satisfy the craving I have. He kisses from my lips, over my jaw, and down my neck. I shiver as he trails his tongue over my chest and into the cleavage sticking out of my dress. He won't get much further than that until I'm free from this tight dress.

Mason had already stripped his jacket off and undone his tie and the top few buttons of his shirt before we left the reception. I move my fingers to the buttons on his shirt and get a few undone before he gets on his knees, reaches over his head, and pulls the damn thing off in one swoop. I sit up, peppering kisses over his chest and running my tongue over and between the curves and valleys of his strong, muscled chest. The warm, woodsy scent of his cologne will be etched in my memory, along with this moment, forever. I push his pants and boxer briefs down and take him in my hand as my kisses move down his torso.

Holding him in my hand, inches from my mouth, I look up and see love staring back down at me. I keep my eyes locked on his as I move in, taking his velvet tip into my mouth. His eyes burn into me as I move my head back and forth, pulling him in and out. He gathers my hair, holding it tightly at the base and groaning as I pick up pace, my hand stroking where my mouth can't reach. My other hand wanders his chest, knowing the heart that loves me is underneath. That this man is mine. He loves me. And I believe him. I moan as the thumping in my core begs for attention. Just like he always does, Mason reads me.

He pulls himself back slowly, leans down, and places a quick kiss on my lips. He kicks his pants the rest of the way off, and the belt buckle clanks on the floor. The beat from outside changes to a fast-paced dance song, and Mason's feral eyes rake over my body.

"This is the hottest fucking dress I've ever seen." He licks his lip as he grabs both sides of the slit in my dress. "But I want it…" The sound of ripping fabric and my gasp ricochets through the small bedroom as he rips my dress from the slit all the way up. "Off." He grabs the spaghetti straps and snaps them off one by one.

"How the hell did you just do that?" I ask, unbelieving it just happened.

He moves over me, pressing his skin against mine until I feel his breath against my lips. "Nothing will ever come between us." He kisses me. "This," he says, holding up the torn fabric, "was in my way."

A wicked grin crosses his face, and he plants his mouth into my chest, working his tongue and lips over each breast. His hand grazes my side until it reaches my hip, and I suck in a small breath, knowing the relief I've been yearning for is coming. Anticipating his touch at my core, my hips move just as he reaches me. A growl from deep inside of him radiates through me as he finds me soaking and swirls his fingertips around the sensitive bud before sinking into me.

"Mason," I whisper, holding on to him, never wanting to lose this feeling. He works his fingers as his kisses, suckles, and licks move closer and closer to his hand. I'm not sure I'll be able to take any more of this. The buildup is too strong. His rhythm is too good. I barely hang on until his mouth encloses around my clit, and I skyrocket into climax. My body trembles as his fingers and mouth are relentless on my body. My legs shutter around his head as I grab the pillow from under my head and cover my face with it. Mason grabs the pillow and throws it across the room. I tilt my head and see his eyes penetrate mine with a hunger I've never seen in him. My moans bounce off the walls as he continues until I pull on his head, desperate for him to be inside. Desperate to be one.

"Fuck," he says, breathless. "Condoms in the other room."

"I don't care," I say, pulling him. "I'm on birth control, and I trust you." I do. I trust Mason with everything. My heart. My soul. My life. "I trust you."

He smashes his lips onto mine. "I trust you too." He lines himself up with my entrance, and I inhale sharply as he works himself in, filling me. "Oh God, Andi. You feel…"

"So fucking good," I say, finishing his sentence for him. He hovers over me as he slowly pumps in and out. This is new. The other times we've had sex, it's been fast and fun. Exciting. This is different. This is love. And it's so strong and deliberate. He's right. Nothing can break this. I rock my hips to match his controlled pace, feeling every groove along my inside, rubbing against nerve endings I didn't even know I had. I pant as he thrusts once a little harder than he has been, but his rhythm returns to the painfully delicious slow pumps.

A bead of sweat on his forehead catches the light just before he kisses me again. His tongue moves in my mouth deep and slow. As if the torture below wasn't enough. I can't keep track of how many times the songs have changed, but the beat kicks up again. Mason breaks our kiss and pulls his head back enough to take in my face. Then he pulls his hips back and thrusts into me, my mouth falling open as I cry out in pleasure. He thrusts again and doesn't stop. He watches me as my body shakes with every glorious drive. I know it's coming.

The surge starts deep inside of me, working its way to the surface, and with one of his deep plunges, I explode around him, grabbing any part of him I can hold on to as I come undone. With one hand wrapped around the back of his neck and the other holding on to his arm, my body convulses as he continues his pace. I wrap my legs around his waist, allowing him to get as deep as he can as I call his name. He rocks into me a few more times before he buries himself in deep and holds himself there.

"Oh God, Andi," he growls in my ear as he twitches inside of me. Leaning on one arm, he presses his cheek against mine until he stills. "Forever. You and me. We're for fucking ever."

Mason's words fill me with so much joy, but I wish I could ignore the pang of fear inside too. We've both been through so much that I'm unsure of what he pictures his future looking like. *What does mine look like?*

He brushes a piece of hair that was fucked out of my updo off my face and touches his lips softly to mine. He winces as he slowly removes himself from me. I hate that I have to get up, but a wet rag isn't going to clean me tonight. I sit up, and Mason holds his hand out to help me from the bed.

"I really want to take a shower with you, but we aren't going to fit in there together," he says, and laughter bursts from us. "You can go first."

"I just need to use the bathroom, but then you can shower first. It's going to take me an hour to get out all the bobby pins I stuck in."

I was right. As Mason comes out of the shower, I'm still picking out pins. With only a towel around his waist, he sits on the bed next to me and starts plucking pins. When the last one comes out, he sinks his hands into my hair and gently rubs my head. I take a fast shower and hop back in bed with Mason. He touches my cheek as I scoot close to his face, both of us on our side. He looks like he has something on his mind, but so do I.

"I want to ask you something, but I don't want to ruin what happened here tonight."

"Ask me. I will always be a person you can say anything to. No matter what it is."

What if I bring this up and it scares him away?

"Do you think you'll ever want to get married?"

If it wasn't for the night-light barely hitting his face from the hallway, I wouldn't have seen the small flinch. But I did.

"Why do you ask that question?" He runs the back of his fingers over my cheek.

Damn. Deflected and perfectly timed. I wasn't sure I'd ever bring this up to anyone again. And even though we just had this beautiful evening making love, this moment between us is important too. He should know everything.

"I was engaged once too." I thought I'd see surprise on his face, but there is none. "I went through the whole shebang. Took me a year to plan down to every last detail. Down to the confetti on the tables at the reception. I had the most gorgeous dress I had ever seen. I cried when I put it on." His mouth shuts tight, and from the shadow it makes, I can see his jaw tick. I try not to cry, even though that day changed who I am as a person. "Like I was a worn-out wet coat, he just hung me to dry. I didn't know he had been cheating on me for the last six months that I was planning our wedding. I thought everything was perfect. Maybe I was just blind, but I had no warning. One day I was the light of his life, and the next, he just left me in the church alone in a white dress." Mason wipes the tear that runs down my cheek away with his thumb. "I'm telling you this because I need you to know I won't survive that again."

"It's hard for people like us. Betrayed by the people we thought we trusted. But I've seen it make so many of my brothers happy beyond their dreams. We don't have to plan anything. As long as we're happy together, we live our lives day by day and let life happen."

And somehow, just as he always does, Mason says exactly the right thing to ease my fears. I kiss his lips, and he pulls me into him. My grandmother's house was always my safe place. But in Mason's arms, I've never felt safer.

―――――

WAKING up next to Mason after the night we had is one of the best sights in the world. The muscles in his face are relaxed as he breathes peacefully. The white bedsheet is draped over his torso, putting his chiseled chest and stomach on display. My hardworking man at rest is a sight I look forward to for years to come. I take my time slithering out of bed, careful not to wake him. I tiptoe out to the tiny living room where my phone is and send a quick text to Jessica. By the time I use the bathroom and get back to my phone, she's sent a text back. Knowing the diner is up and running the way it should be gives me the peace I need to go back to bed with Mason. As I enter the room, I spot the evidence of passion on the floor. I pick up the shreds of gorgeous emerald green that used to make up my dress.

"I'll buy you a new dress," Mason says, his morning voice gruff and doing something to me inside. I smile and let the fabric fall back to the floor and climb back under the covers.

"I don't go anywhere to need a new dress," I laugh.

"Why are you up so early?"

"I can't relax until I know the diner is taken care of. I texted Jessica, and she said everything is perfect."

"Good. Does this mean we get morning lovin' too?"

I giggle as he slides his hand under the sheets and grazes my side on his way to my ass. Just as he rolls on top of me, his phone rings from the living room. He ignores it as he takes my lips, and I feel his erection growing against me. The ringing starts again, and he growls.

"I have to answer that. Just in case something is wrong." He jumps out of bed. "Someone better be dying," he groans, and I watch his naked ass walk out of the bedroom.

I lean into his pillow, and it smells like his cedarwood shampoo. He walks back in with his phone in his hand. "Breakfast is done up at the house."

"I guess we have to get up, then." I sit up and let the sheet fall as I stretch.

Mason drops his phone to the ground and leaps onto the bed. "There's only one thing I'm hungry for, and it ain't pancakes."

————

MASON and I walk into Owen and Natalie's house. I was in here a few times before when I was at the lodge for Tana and Lucas's wedding. It's a gorgeous home filled with warm woods and cozy cream accents. I think it could be the most welcoming home I've ever stepped foot in. As Mason holds my hand, we walk into the living room, and Tana calls my name from the kitchen.

"The guys are out back, Mas," Natalie says, Starling wriggling in her arms.

Mason walks me to the kitchen, brings my hand up to his lips, and kisses it. He smiles at me as he gently drops my hand, nods at the ladies, and walks out of the room. Tana and Natalie stare at me as I take a seat next to Tana, who's cradling a cup of coffee in her hand.

"Want a cup?" Natalie asks, finally breaking the silence.

"I would love one. I'm exhausted." I close my eyes the moment the words cross my lips.

"Oh really. I would have no idea why," Tana chimes in, and

her sarcastic tone makes me laugh. "I mean, judging by the time you left the reception, you should be well rested," Tana says.

"Oh, stop giving her a hard time," Natalie says, handing me a cup. "There's cream in the fridge and sugar right there on the counter if you'd like it."

"I'm good just the way it is, thank you." I take a slurping sip of the hot liquid and can't wait until the caffeine enters my system. I was paying attention to the coffee and not the fact that Tana and Natalie are both staring at me. "What?"

"Not what," Tana says, putting her cup down and crossing her arms. "That man is in love with you."

"I know," I say, trying to avoid talking by taking another sip.

Natalie moves closer with her mouth hanging open. "You love him too."

"It's about damn time the two of you stop pretending. You've been in love with each other for months. Lucas and I were taking bets on how long this was going to last before you both got out of denial."

Tana is my best friend, and I know she saw through all of my walls a long time ago. "Love is scary."

"Of course it is," Natalie says, and the baby starts to fuss in her arms. "It's giving someone else access to everything that makes you who you are."

Tana puts her hand over mine on the table. "I don't think love is scary. It's people who take that love for granted who are scary. You aren't around people who do that. And I'm pretty sure Mason would kill anyone who ever tried to hurt you."

"Didn't he already almost do that?" Natalie asks, bouncing Starling.

"Oh yeah." Tana's grin gets even wider. "Thank God there were people around, including Tucker, because he wasn't stopping."

"How did he not get arrested?" I ask, shaking my head.

"According to Lucas, you started yelling at him, and damn near the whole town saw what was happening. Those country boys don't mess around when it comes to stuff like that. If Mason wouldn't have gotten to him first with Lucas right behind him, there were about ten other guys ready to do it too. None of them were about to call the police. They had it handled."

Starling's cries get more frantic, and all the attention turns to her. "Can one of you hold her while I make her bottle up?" Natalie asks, but I'm the closest, and she starts handing the baby to me.

"I, uh...I don't think you want me to hold her. Babies usually cry when I hold them."

"Well, she's already crying, so," Natalie says, laughing as I take Starling in my arms and stand up from the chair. I've never done well with babies. Probably because I've never really been around them. I sway back and forth and hum the tune my daddy used to help me calm down when I was little. Starling opens her eyes and looks up at me as her wails quiet and her body tries to ease her hiccupped breaths. My eyes widen as I smile wide.

"Um, so you're never leaving," Natalie says, and we all start laughing. Except one person. The man who has walked into the kitchen and is standing frozen just inside the doorway, his eyes stuck on me.

"Mason? You okay?" I ask. "Look what I did," I say proudly.

Without taking his eyes off mine, he speaks. "Owen needs a tape measure."

Natalie grabs one from the drawer and hands it to Mason, and he peels his attention off me. "Thanks."

Once the back sliding door closes, Tana and Natalie erupt. "Holy shit. You're in trouble, girl," Natalie says.

"Yep. I've seen that look before."

"What was that look?" I ask.

Tana's smile fades. "That look says he's in it for life with you.

Make no mistake on that."

"Yep," Natalie says. "You better give us enough time to recoup from this wedding before we have yours out here."

I laugh before I realize I'm laughing. "I don't think you have to worry about that."

———

AFTER A LONG CAR RIDE, Mason walks me into my dark house. He flips on the lights as he moves from the living room to the kitchen.

"I'll put your bags in your room for you," he says, taking the only small one he would let me carry out of my hand. I know what he's doing, and he doesn't even try to hide it as he opens and looks in the spare room, the bathroom, and my bedroom. My man is making sure my house is safe.

It feels good to be home. I flop down on the couch and grab my beloved cozy blanket. I can't wait to light the candles and watch a movie. I love the people I surround myself with, including all of Mason's friends too. But I need a little downtime to recharge from people. Except Mason. I never feel like I need to be away from him.

He saunters into the room from the hallway, obviously relaxed now that he's searched my house for God knows what. I tap the couch, and he sits down next to me. I want him to stay, but I know he'll do it even though he shouldn't.

"What time do you have to be at work tomorrow?"

He groans and runs his hand over his face. "Sunrise."

"Damn," I say. "I guess it's probably not a good idea for you to stay the night."

"Do not play with me. If you want me here, I'm here. There's an alarm on my phone that works just fine."

I take a deep breath. "I can't have you falling off the roof like

Lucas did. And if you stay here, we both know you won't be getting any sleep tonight."

"I'll sleep when I'm dead."

I laugh when something pops into my head. "Why don't you ever invite me to your house?"

"Because my house is just four walls with some paint. This house has soul. Yours. You are free to come to my house anytime you want. Say the word and we can stay there. But I notice how different your eyes are when we're anywhere other than here. You're alive in this house, and I don't want anything to do with taking that shine out of you."

Unable to gather my own thoughts, my heart pounds at how much I love this man. How he knows me so well and loves me for exactly who I am. I didn't have to explain it to him. He just gets it. "I love you, Mason."

He moves closer and presses his full lips to mine in one deep, passionate kiss. "I love you too." The hesitation is all over his face, but he gets up from the couch anyway. I follow him to the door.

"I'm only two streets away if you need me."

I laugh. "I know where you live, Mason."

"Good night, babe."

"Night."

He gives me one more kiss, touches my cheek, and walks out. I close the door and double-check the lock.

I head to my bedroom and take all the clothes out of my overnight bags. I grab a laundry basket and throw them in. Since the diner is closed tomorrow, I'll worry about them then. But I can't relax until my things are put away. My nightstand looks empty when I remember my charger is in my purse. I jog to the kitchen, open my purse, and grab my charger and my phone. When my finger touches the screen, I see a few missed calls from Jessica and a text message.

JESSICA: I'm so sorry. I left that coffee pot on in your office. I went out of town for the night with my mom so I can't go back to turn it off.

Shit. I don't tell a lot of people about the coffeepot I have hidden on a low shelf behind my desk. I'm supposed to love the coffee that is served at my own diner. The problem is, I had an issue with my coffee distributor, and I haven't found one I've liked since. I'm determined to have the best coffee in the county, I just have to keep looking. Until then, I'll brew my own in my office in a diner mug, and none will be the wiser. The only people who know are Tana and Jessica since they work in the office when I'm not there. Luckily, we drove past the diner on our way home, so I know it hasn't burnt to the ground. I text back.

ANDI: Don't worry about it. I'll go shut it off right now. Have fun on your trip.

All I want to do is change into my pajamas and snuggle up in the living room. Instead, I shove my phone back into my purse, sling it over my shoulder, and grab my keys. It's only a minute drive to the diner, and as I park in the back, I'm thankful for the cameras Mason set up. I used to be super creeped out back here in the dark. This will only take a minute. I jump out of my car and make my way into the diner. The lights are all off except for the few dim ones that stay on all the time in the front dining room. I walk into my office and flip on the switch, and the door slams behind me.

"Hello, Andrea Taylor." Ice-cold fear runs through every vein that was just set on fire by Mason. I know that voice. "I think you should have a *fucking* seat."

CHAPTER THIRTEEN

MASON

I WANTED to stay longer at Andi's, but I know her well enough to see how exhausted she was. And it wasn't just because we didn't get much sleep. Being around people drains her, and I never want to be part of that group. When she wants me, I'll run through fire to get to her. But I know she needs a little space, and I'm always going to give her what she needs.

My phone rings from the table next to my chair in the living room.

I pick it up and see Lucas's name on the screen. "Hey, Lucas," I answer.

"Are you busy?"

"Not at all. Just sitting at home by myself."

"What? Is something wrong between you and Andi?"

I already know Tana filled him in on all the juicy details on their ride back home from the lodge. "Andi told me if I stayed, I would be so tired that I'd fall off the roof like you did. So thanks for falling of the roof and fucking up my night."

Lucas laughs on the other end. "Yeah, I did that. Anyway, I could've waited to talk to you about this tomorrow, but it's kind of fucking with my brain."

"What's wrong, brother?"

"Lenny sat me down when we got home this afternoon and told me he wants to retire."

Lenny has been with Lucas since he started working at the roofing company under the old owner when he got out of prison. When Lucas took over the business, Lenny became his mentor and the guy in charge when Lucas isn't there. He also became family when he started dating Tana's mama.

"You had to know it was coming, right?"

"I did, but now I need someone to take his supervisor position. Someone I trust with my life. You. Do you want it?"

Taking on this position brings a lot more responsibility and a few more tasks that I'll have to learn, but I already know how to run the rest of it.

"Does this mean I don't get to work with you every day anymore?"

"Unfortunately for you, you're stuck with me. I'm not getting up on a roof with anyone else."

"Then I appreciate it, and yes. I'll take the job."

"Thank fuck. See you in the morning."

"Bright and early," I say and hang up.

It wasn't long ago that I wasn't sure if I wanted to stay in Cresna. Lucas was the only thing that saved me after I got out of prison. But it was hard to watch all of my friends settle down and make a life for themselves when I didn't think that was in the cards for me. It's one of the reasons I bought my fifth wheel camper. I could pick up and leave anytime I wanted to, and I was getting damn close to doing it. Now, my entire world is lit up by Andi, and I have this amazing job to support her. Life is as close to perfect as it could be.

With my phone still in my hand, I text Andi the good news.

MASON: I was just offered the supervisor position at work. Nothing could spoil the weekend. It was one of the best of my life.

A few minutes pass before those bouncing dots appear.

ANDI: So awesome! Talk later.
MASON: You okay?
ANDI: Yep. Just tired.
MASON: Talk to you tomorrow. I love you.
ANDI: Love you too.

I stare at the words on the screen. Maybe my paranoia is kicking in, but that conversation didn't seem like her.

CHAPTER FOURTEEN

Andi

AN EVIL, dark cloud ascends on this man's face as he grins. He tosses my phone onto my desk in front of me. I know it was Mason who texted me. Please let him realize something is wrong. *Help me. I need you.* As if he's going to get some sixth sense and pick up my internal cries for him like they do on TV.

If only I could reach my phone, but the zip ties holding my wrists to the armrests of my office chair are already biting into my skin. The room doesn't smell like the typical roasting coffee beans. There isn't a waft of chili coming from the kitchen. It's not warm like it is when the diner is full of people moving about. It's cold, sterile, and dark.

His dark brown beard covers his chin and upper lip and matches the short hair on his head. He's dressed in a black button-up collared shirt, black pants, and black dress shoes. His gold watch peeks out from his sleeve that's adorned with expensive-looking cufflinks. I'm not sure if he's in the mafia, going to a funeral, or trying to go unseen in the night sky. But the scariest accessory on him is the gun clipped to his belt. He taps on his chin as he paces the room.

"Why are you doing this?"

He ignores my question and sits in the chair on the other side of the desk. I feel sick as he stares at me with a hatred I've never felt before. He's been in the diner a lot lately and barely eats anything. Tana says he usually orders a coffee, two pieces of toast, and one egg. Who eats one egg? And as far as I know, there were only two houses up for sale in Cresna the entire last year, and I've already met the new people in town. If he isn't a local, why is he traveling to this little country town to eat one egg and have some shitty coffee?

"Who are you?" I ask.

I hate how attractive he is when he smiles wide with perfect, bright white teeth. Though he won't be once Mason gets a hold of him.

"Word of advice," he says, leaning back in the chair and crossing his hands across his torso. "You might want to lock your office door when you aren't in it."

"That's not how it works around here. I trust my employees. Why would I lock it?"

A chill runs down my spine as his creep level rises with every smug smirk. "Because someone might be able to take something from you."

"Take something from me? What the hell are you talking about?"

He reaches onto my desk where he tossed the rest of my things when he ripped them from my hands and picks up my car keys. He flips through the ring until he finds one that brings this whole thing to an even scarier reality. My house key.

"You keep a very clean home, Ms. Taylor."

"How did you…"

"Very easily. You trust too much. I walked right into this

office, took a photo of your house key and the diner key. I mean, I didn't even have to try," he laughs. "Did you know that? You can make a whole new key and have it sent straight to your house… well, my house…with just a cell phone app. That's so creepy, isn't it?" This man is not mentally stable, and the more he speaks, the more obvious that becomes.

"Why?" I ask, my voice full of terror.

"This town is pretty amazing. So much drama. Like your friend Bobby. Ompf," he says, his face covered in sarcasm. "Now that was fun to watch. Although I'm a little disappointed in how the evening turned out at the Fall Fest. I was hoping for so much more."

The large knot in my stomach is twisting and turning the more he talks. He was in my house. He saw me at the Fall Fest and what Bobby did. "You're disappointed he didn't get away with assaulting me?"

"He's still alive, which made it a little boring, no?"

"Who are you?" I ask, disgusted.

"That doesn't matter…yet. What does matter is how fucking stunning you were in that green dress at the shop in Birkenshire." He slides his tongue along his bottom lip. "You could be a model. You know that? I used to be a professional photographer for one of the most prestigious modeling agencies in New York."

He's a crazed lunatic. "You've been watching me?"

"I'm so glad you decided against that bright red nail polish and chose the soft pink instead. It suits your skin tone so much better."

It gets harder to breathe as he reveals just how long he's been watching me. At least since Tana and I went to the salon, and that was a while ago already. He's just been sitting in the shadows.

"All those times, I felt like someone was watching me. It was you." My throat burns from screaming when I first arrived.

Mason told me Owen always checks the cameras before he goes to bed at night. *Please let him go to bed early tonight.*

The devil shines in his eyes. "It was me."

"What were you doing in my house? What could you possibly want with me?" I beg for answers.

"I'm quite thirsty. Are you thirsty? Your voice sounds hoarse. I'm going to get a drink. I'd be happy to get you one too." His casual tone sends shivers down my spine, but I can't seem to keep my attitude in check.

"I'm not thirsty, and no, you can't have one. Now, get the hell out of my diner."

"Tsk, tsk. I'll be right back. Sit tight." He laughs as he rises from the chair and shoves all of my things further from my reach, as if I could get my hands free anyway. He walks out of the room and returns a minute later, sipping from a straw in a cup of water. "So refreshing. Here." He walks to me and holds the straw he just used up to my lips.

"I said no."

"C'mon. Stop being difficult, just take a drink. I don't want you." I want to slit this man's throat and feed him to Mason afterward. But the only thing I can do is suck on the straw and pull a large amount of water into my mouth. I twist my head, freeing my lips from the straw, tilt back, and spit the water into his face.

"Fuck you," I say through gritted teeth.

Emotionless, he stands in front of me, water dripping down his face, staring. I won't sit here like a lamb. I wasn't reassembled that way. I don't know what he wants from me, but I'm not going down quietly. The years of battle I have already fought to be a stronger woman are not going to fail me tonight. I'm going to find a way out of this. *Whatever this is.*

He finally breaks his demonic stare and stands up, sets the glass on the table, and wipes his face with his hand.

"You're delightful." His monotone voice is just as creepy as he is as he sits back down across from me only to stare some more. It feels like several minutes have passed before he swallows and moves his eyes away from mine.

"Did you have a nice visit with your parents? I wasn't expecting your mom to be so goddamn hot. Wow."

Adrenaline spikes in my bloodstream. "You shut your fucking mouth."

"Or what?"

"The second I get out of this chair…" His boom of laughter cuts me off, and I want to cry, but I hold it in.

"I'm not worried," he says, amusement dripping from his words. He reaches over the desk and grabs my phone again. He holds it up to my face to unlock it, sits back in the chair, and from the motion of his hand, he's scrolling through something.

"Please. Will you just tell me what the hell you want?" At least if I knew, there would be answers. But the longer I don't get them, the more confused and frightened I am.

"Aw, this is such a cute picture of the two of you." He turns my phone and shows me a picture of Mason and me at Everest's wedding. Mason isn't looking at the camera because his eyes are so focused on me. It's my favorite picture Tana took all night. I remember wishing just once, someone would look at me the way Mason does. I've never felt so adored. "Too bad you won't get to take another one together."

My heart stops. "What does that mean? Are you going to kill me?" The words come out broken because I can't find the breath inside of me to push them all out.

"Shhh." He puts his finger over his lips. "I don't want to hurt you, Andrea."

"Then for the love of God, will you please tell me what the hell you're doing here?" He only grins, and my fear starts to manifest into rage. "What the fuck do you want," I scream. He bolts forward, slamming my phone onto the desk, cracking the screen. The tears are uncontrollable any longer. "What do you want?" I ask again.

"Revenge," he growls.

"What could I have possibly done to deserve this?"

"Fuck," he whispers to himself, inspecting the shattered phone screen. "You idiot."

Great, now he's calling himself names. Of course I would attract a lunatic in this tiny town and somehow get mixed up in this. He pulls another phone from his pocket. It's light blue and has little sparkly rhinestones in the shape of a *J* on the case. *Jessica's phone.*

"Where is Jessica?"

"What? Oh, the phone. You people are seriously way too trusting around here. Things are just left everywhere. I mean, everything has been damn near handed to me."

"Where. Is. She?"

"How the hell should I know? I haven't seen her since I took her phone off the counter by the register this morning." I swallow that lump in my throat, knowing she's probably home safe, thinking she lost her phone. But the relief is temporary as I'm still here with a madman. He taps on my screen a few times, and Jessica's phone chirps. "Oh good. Your phone still works. You know, you might want to let her know that keeping the code for the alarm system isn't the best idea."

Oh my God. I was too busy freaking out about being tied up that it never even occurred to me the alarm wasn't sounding. He stole Jessica's phone, got into the diner, shut off the alarm, and lured me here, pretending to be her. He waited in this office for his time to strike. And since he's been following me, he knew exactly when Mason left and when to send that text message.

"You just wait until Mason figures out I'm in here. You may as well dig your own grave now. He's going to kill you."

The deep laughter from his belly fills the room, and I want to throw up, but I continue to cry instead.

"I think it's time to speed this up." He sets Jessica's phone down and taps rapidly on my broken phone screen. "And send. There. Now we wait."

"Wait for what?" My body trembles, and the shaking causes the zip ties to cut my skin.

He holds the phone up to me, and I read the text he just sent to Mason.

MEET ME IN THE DINER IN FIFTEEN MINUTES. I HAVE A SURPRISE FOR YOU IN MY OFFICE.

The three bouncing bubbles appear, but he takes the phone away before I can see what Mason's response is. Not like I need to. I know he's coming. But he's going to be caught off guard.

"Oh goody," he says, standing from the chair. "The show is about to begin."

"Please, just tell me why. Why me?" He puts both phones in one hand and rubs his forehead with the other.

"God, you are a conceited little bitch, aren't you?" He walks around the desk, puts the phones on the edge, and turns my chair. Sweat forms in the palms of my hands as he leans down and gets close to my face with stern eyes. "Not everything is about you," he yells, pushing the papers on my desk with such force they fly everywhere. He slowly stands, swipes his shirt a few times to straighten it, and looks at me with disgust. "Now, if you'll just shut the hell up, I have to prepare." He slams his hand down on the phone, picks it up, and sticks it in his pocket without taking his eyes off me. "One more sound out of you and I'll tape your mouth shut."

He grabs the gun from his waistband, and a whimper comes from deep in my chest as I try to control the tears falling from my eyes. I watch him walk out of my office, and I have to do something. He's going to shoot Mason. I dart my eyes around the desk, desperate for an idea of how to break free when I spot it. My phone.

The idiot grabbed Jessica's phone and forgot about mine because it's mostly hidden under a paper that must have fallen on it when he sent them all flying. It's my only chance. I use my feet to move the chair forward just enough that I can lean over and blow the paper off the phone. On the second try, I catch the screen with my chin and drag the phone closer to the edge of the desk. The text message is still up, which stopped my phone from locking.

Pain shoots through my shoulders as I push far enough forward to tap the screen with my nose. I hit a few keys before I hit the image of the two of us at the wedding and it brings up the button to call him. Again, I tap the screen with my nose and allow the sobs to come as the phone begins to call Mason. I can't hear that he picked up, but the call timer shows he did.

"Don't come," I try to whisper quiet enough not to be heard by the crazy man but loud enough for my love to hear me. The man's dress shoes come charging down the hall. "He's got a gun," I say louder. It doesn't matter. He already knows I'm talking to someone. "Mason, don't come here. Get Tuck—"

He grabs the phone and ends the call. "You fucking bitch." My cheek stings as his open hand smacks across my skin. "You're ruining everything. He's supposed to walk in, I shoot him, and you die inside. That was the plan." The calm villain is gone. This one is losing his mind. He roughly runs his hands through his hair, moving each piece out of its gelled position, making some stick straight up. "He knows. God dammit, he knows. He'll be prepared now." His shoes ping on the floor as he paces before he turns his head to me and lifts the gun. "Maybe the plans will have to change."

CHAPTER FIFTEEN

MASON

HER WORDS POUND in my ears as I continue to scream her name into the phone. I can't feel the floor under my feet as I race to my bedroom. I open my nightstand and press my finger onto the fingerprint scanner. My gun safe opens, and I snatch my gun, run to the kitchen, grab my keys from the hook, and run out of the house. My fingers tremble as I scroll to Tucker's name as I throw myself into the driver's seat and start the car.

"What's up, Mason?"

"Someone has Andi at the diner with a gun," I say, breathless.

"I'm on my way. Do not go in there, Mason. You stay the fuck out of that diner until I get there. You hear me?"

I heard him, but I hang up the phone as my tires peel out on the pavement. He knows me better than that. Nothing is going to stop me from going into that diner and burying the motherfucker who dares touch her. I want to call Lucas for more backup. I want to call Owen to check the cameras. But there just isn't any time.

There's fear because something startles you or you're worried about the future. Then there's this fear. The mind-numbing, body-on-fire terror that enters your soul when you know your life can change in the next five minutes. Not one hair on her head better be out of place. I pull up half a block down from the diner and shut my car off. The last thing I want to do is come roaring into the parking lot, giving the maniac advanced notice that I've arrived. The sound of the rocks shifting under my feet as I leap out of my car and start running to the diner is amplified by the silence of the town around me.

No one has a clue that right next door, a fucking crazy person is holding Andi hostage in the diner they just had biscuits and gravy in hours earlier. And if God forbid something happens to her, they'll all mourn her for a week and then go about their lives. But mine will be forever changed. My heart will never recover.

I pull out my gun and silently open the back door. The only lights in the diner are the few in the dining room down the hall and one bright one shining out from Andi's office. I pull my gun up and slide my back against the wall as I tiptoe toward the open door. The sound of Andi's muffled sobs both break me and fill me with relief. I know she's alive, but I'm about to fucking end whoever is putting those tears on her face. I spin, looking in through the doorway, gun drawn. Her office chair is facing away, but it suddenly spins around, and I'm convinced my eyes are deceiving me.

"Kenneth?"

"Hello," he says, drawing out each sound. "You might want to lower that." He wags his finger at my gun, and I laugh. "No, really." He nods at his side, and Andi rises from behind the desk. Kenneth's other hand that was under the desk is holding a gun, and it's pointed right at my girl. Her hands are tied in front of her and are as red as her face from crying. There's a line of blood on the tip of her nose and an outline of a hand on her cheek. *He hit her. He's a fucking dead man.* A hurricane rages inside of me.

Once I get Andi out of here, I will have no remorse. But she can't see that. She's not like me. It would darken her shine with evil.

"What the fuck do you want, Kenneth?"

"First, put it down." He wiggles the gun at Andi, and I slowly lower my weapon to the floor. "Kick it away."

I'm not fucking stupid. I kick it behind me and down the hall, knowing Tucker and hopefully some backup is about to come in here. There's no way I'm giving him access to two guns.

"Not ideal, but acceptable. Please, come on in."

I watch his eye movements, predicting his next step. "Let her go. This is between us."

"It was all him, Mason," Andi says, the tears streaming down her face. "He was in my house."

Kenneth's proud grin makes me want to break out each one of his teeth. "Except the 'I hate you' letter. That one was for you, Mason," he says, blinking rapidly. He's lost it.

"Where's Arianna? Didn't you two get married, have a couple kids, and live your lives of infidelity together? Not like I give a fuck."

His face falls. "No," he spits out. "No, that didn't happen. Thanks to you."

The angrier he gets, the more he'll make mistakes. Movement from the corner of my eye brings a small bit of relief. Knowing I could give away Tucker's position, I keep my eyes focused on Kenneth.

"Good. I had hoped you were both fucking miserable."

His shoulders rise and fall at a rapid pace as the rage inside of him boils. I welcome it. As long as he keeps that on me. I take tiny steps further and further into the corner of the office, and as hoped, his eyes and body turn to follow me. I need to give Andi a clear path out of the office.

"It's because of you." Spit flies from his mouth when he speaks. "You did it. It's your fault I lost her."

"It's my fault that you fucked my fiancée in my bed?"

"She felt so guilty that you went to prison over what she did that she couldn't stand to be with me anymore."

"Oh, how sad. Remind me to send her a feel-better-soon card. You can just go fuck yourself."

He swings the gun in my direction, and I keep the digs up, buying time and keeping his attention off her. Taking notes from me, my smart girl takes tiny steps, putting herself further behind Kenneth. If she can get directly behind him, it won't be easy for him to swing around and aim at her.

"How dare you," Kenneth snaps. "You have no idea how you've ruined my entire life. I had everything when I was with her, and you destroyed it. You destroyed her."

"No, she destroyed herself. And you're just the idiot who thought you could keep her."

Andi slides on a sheet of paper and falls to the floor. He spins around, and I move. The world becomes a blur in the midst of wrestling with the gun in Kenneth's hand.

"Mason, be careful," Tucker yells.

"Grab Andi," I yell back, wrestling Kenneth to the ground.

Tucker drags Andi out of the office. Kenneth has a hard grip on the gun that's smashed between our bodies. But my hands are on it too.

The gun goes off.

"Mason!" Tucker yells.

Andi screams.

And time stops.

CHAPTER SIXTEEN

Andi

UNTIL HIS EYES HIT MINE, a part of me feels dead. The officer's hands hold my arms tightly as I cry and fight to get into that room. I need to know he's okay. This can't be how this ends. Our life together has only just begun. Tucker went into the office what feels like hours ago and has yet to call for help or let me go in.

"Mason!" My throat burns from screaming his name, but I won't stop until I see him. Tucker appears in the doorway, his face aimed at the ground. My body stills as he leans against the wall, and Mason stumbles out, his clothes painted in crimson. Tucker nods at the sheriff holding me back, and the second he lets me go, I run from the dining room to Mason.

"Oh my God," I sob, running my hands over his body. "Where are you hurt? Is an ambulance coming? Are you shot?"

He grabs my frantic hands. "It's not my blood, babe. I'm fine."

"Where is this blood coming from?" I ask, pulling my hands out of his and lifting his shirt. "Tucker? Is there an ambulance coming for Mason?" I shout, and he shares a look with Mason before stepping to the side with the other officers.

"Andi, I'm okay. I promise. I'm not bleeding."

"Are you sure?"

He nods, takes a small step back, tugs his red-stained shirt off his body, and tosses it to the ground. He pulls me into his arms, and my feet leave the ground as he picks me up and carries me to one of the booths in the dining room. I sob as he holds me hard against him. "Jesus. Are you all right, babe?"

I can't stop shaking. The sound of the gun is something that will haunt me for the rest of my life. "Is he…"

"He's not going to bother us anymore."

"Oh my God." The sobs continue so hard my chest hurts. "Are you going to be in trouble? Are they going to take you away?" I pull him tighter to me.

"Mason isn't going anywhere," Tucker says, walking up to us. "I saw everything, and the sheriff was behind me. We know what happened in there. You saved her, man." He slaps Mason's shoulder. "Do you hurt anywhere, Andi? I think you should get checked out."

"No. I'm fine. Just a few scrapes and a nightmare I won't be able to rid myself of."

"Fuck," Mason whispers and puts his hand on my head as I nuzzle into his neck.

"In my diner." Everything is just too much, and my body feels like it's shutting down. "I feel like I can't breathe."

"I'm going to take her outside in the fresh air, Tuck."

"Go on ahead. You just can't leave yet. Unfortunately, we're going to need you here for statements and access to the cameras."

I rest my head on Mason's chest, his heart racing a thousand beats a minute. He's acting calm and collected, but I feel how worked up he is. A loud truck speeds up to the diner, shooting gravel before sliding to a stop. The door opens, and Lucas runs to the front door of the diner.

"What the fuck?" he shouts as he runs to us and puts a hand on Mason's shoulder. He runs his eyes over me.

"How did you know?" Mason asks him.

"I got a call from Owen that he saw you on the camera running into the diner with a gun in your hand. He just happened to glance at it the same time you came into the frame."

"We found out who was in Andi's house. He lured her here." My stomach turns as he explains the evening to Lucas.

A cold, sinister glare takes over Lucas's eyes. "Where is that motherfucker?" He starts looking around the diner.

"Let's go outside. Andi needs some fresh air. I'll explain out there."

Mason carries me outside, and I wait until the cool night air hits my face before I open my eyes. I don't want to see the shambles and chaos my diner is in.

"Put her in my truck," Lucas says, and Mason places me sideways on the driver's seat with my legs hanging out the door.

"I'm going to step right over there to talk to Lucas," he says. I clutch his arms. "Babe, you are safe. I will be five feet away, and you'll be able to see me the entire time. But I have to talk to Lucas."

I nod, and he places a kiss on my lips. Lucas reaches into the back seat, pulls out a shirt, and hands it to Mason. He puts it on, and I wish he hadn't. I can't see his bullet-free skin anymore. Lucas crosses his arms as Mason speaks, but it only lasts for a second before Lucas shoots a look at me, then tries to barge into the diner.

"Woah, brother," Mason says, getting in front of him and pushing against his chest. "She's fine. I'm fine." Lucas relaxes and moves back a few feet. He pulls his phone from his pocket, scrolls his finger over the screen, and hands it to Mason. I don't know who Mason is talking to, but I'm glad his voice is quiet enough so I don't have to listen to the replay.

There's movement all around the diner for hours, but it's all distorted. The paramedics check me and Mason out, we each give our statement, and I was asked if I'm doing okay at least a million times as the officers work "the crime scene." Thank God Tucker was involved in this from the beginning when my front door was open. And for the cameras Mason set up.

The sky is two shades lighter before Mason pulls into the driveway of my house. He opens his door, but I can't seem to move.

"Hey," he says, his voice smooth and soft. "I'm right here."

"I don't want to go in." The tears flood my eyes, like they have all night. "It's all tarnished. My grandmother's home. My diner. He ruined it. I don't want to go in."

"Listen to me," Mason says, putting his finger under my chin and turning my eyes to his. "We don't have to do anything you don't want to do."

"I don't want to go in."

He shuts his door, turns the car back on, and drives two streets over. He's the last house on the street with a huge yard and a large metal garage. I always laughed that his garage was bigger than the house. He pulls into the driveway, shuts off his car, and grabs my hand.

"You're going to stay here with me. For today, the next week, or forever. That is up to you. But for now, we worry about this minute. And right now, in this moment, babe, we're okay."

"He said he wanted me to die inside when he shot you." He kisses the back of my hand and wipes my tear-soaked cheeks with his thumb. "What kind of monster thinks like that?"

"You answered your own question. A monster. But that monster is dead. I'm here, and so are you. Let's go inside, babe."

He gets out, walks around the front of the car, and helps me out. My lips tremble against his, the kiss bringing me a small piece of liberation. It will take a long time to adjust and come to terms with what happened. But I'm going to take Mason's advice. He's never steered me wrong. I'm going to focus on the fact that we are both alive and in each other's arms today. His warm hand slides into mine as he leads me up the steps into his small ranch home.

I've been to Mason's house a few times with Tana when she was dropping something off for him, but I've never been inside. Mason opens the front door, I step inside, and he closes and locks it behind me. The sound from the TV echoes against the bare walls. The only other things in the living room are a couch and a coffee table. It's clean, and I'm taken aback by the smell of warm apple pie.

"It smells good," I say, still sniffling. I kick my shoes off and take a seat on the couch. I don't trust my legs anymore.

"Tana bought me these things that plug into the wall and put scent out. She said it smelled like a guy before, and thinking about that now, I probably should have been more offended." He chuckles, but I know Mason, and it wasn't his usual lighthearted sound. He empties his pockets onto the small island between the kitchen and living room. "I'm going to grab something from my bedroom. Are you okay?"

"Yeah, I'm good." He grins, and I know he believes my words. It does feel good in this house right now. Even though I'm still on edge, I feel safe here.

Mason disappears down the hall, and I stare at the show on TV with burning eyes. I haven't slept in twenty-four hours. A yawn falls from my mouth as Mason walks back into the room.

"It's so nice in here," I say.

"No it isn't," he says, the laugh I'm used to returning. "It's a shell which, to be honest, doesn't really bother me. Now that you're here, I've got everything I could ever need."

"I love you, Mason," I say, connecting my eyes to his as he grabs my hand and helps me from the couch.

"I love you too." He brushes his fingers over the place Kenneth's hand hit my face. His jaw clenches so tight, I'm afraid he'll start cracking teeth.

"I'm all right. I was in a fight once with a girl in high school who hit harder than he did."

"If he wasn't already dead, I'd kill him. C'mon," he says, tugging my hand.

The sound of running water gets louder as we walk down the hall, through his also bare bedroom, and into his master bathroom. Steam coats the mirror, and he closes the door behind us. He wraps his arms around my body as the old claw-foot tub fills with water and bubbles.

"Take bubble baths often with a pink rubber duck?" I ask, nodding to the toy sitting on the corner ledge.

"Oh, that's Mason."

I laugh, and it rattles my sore head, but I welcome the distraction. "There seems to be a lot of Masons running around this town."

He grins proudly. "One time a few months ago when Lucas brought Iris over, she gave it to me. She marched all the way back here, set it on my tub, and forbade me from removing it. So this is *Mason's* home now."

"That girl is precious."

"She is. But if you don't get in that tub soon, the water is going to overflow, knocking Mason right off, and then we'll both be in trouble."

I giggle, and he kisses me tenderly. With a gentle touch, he lifts my shirt over my head, unclasps my bra, and shimmies off my shorts and underwear. He holds my hand as he guides me into the warm water. I take a deep breath and settle against the back of the tub.

He moves to the separate shower and turns the water on. "You're not coming in here with me?"

"I am. I just need to…rinse off first." He glances at his hands that still have remnants of the violence that took place last night. I watch him remove his clothes, inspecting every inch of his body for injury before he goes into the shower and closes the door. Through the frosted glass, I watch as he aggressively scrubs his body. The scent of cedarwood wafts in the air as he washes his hair, rinses the soap out, and shuts off the water. The entire shower took maybe four minutes. I wish I could shower that fast.

He steps out, water dripping from his nose, his nipples, his slight erection. The water splashes out as Mason steps into the tub, leaning his back on the opposite side from me. He adjusts his legs on either side of my body, and I tuck my feet over his hips. I stare at a bubble as the iridescent colors swirl inside of it, dazed.

"Babe," he says, gently rubbing my leg. "Talk to me."

"I heard that shot, I thought I lost you. It was the worst pain I've ever felt in my entire life." A tear falls from my eye.

He leans up and cups my cheek. Mason pulls me in, smashing our naked bodies together and making water go everywhere. "Let that pain go because I'm here, and it's going to take a whole lot more effort to keep me away from you."

CHAPTER SEVENTEEN

Mason

ANDI HASN'T LEFT my house for four days. Tana and Lucas are handling the cleanup at the diner and told Andi she isn't allowed there until they tell her she can come back. Of course, since she owns the place, technically she can show up whenever she wants to. I wasn't sure we were going to be able to keep her away, but she was grateful and hasn't stepped foot in the place since. Especially since she decided to close the diner for two weeks to get it cleaned and repainted.

After she had some rest at my house, I brought her home to gather some necessities. I was hoping she would feel differently about the house once she walked in, but she didn't. And when those tears fell again, I wanted to kill Kenneth all over again. Because the first time wasn't enough.

Kenneth had no chance of overpowering me. For a moment, I was trying to do the right thing. But the second I felt the barrel of the gun start to poke into my chest, I turned it into him, slid my finger over his on the trigger, and shot that motherfucker dead. He fucked up my life once, and truth be told, I'm glad he did. I wouldn't be here with Andi if he hadn't. His grave mistake was coming after *her*.

I park in my driveway and smile at her car parked next to mine. It's the first day I went back to work and felt comfortable leaving her alone. Lucas gave me as much time as I needed, but with him bouncing between getting jobs done and getting the diner back in order, I had to get back to work to help him. I tried to go into the diner to help, and they pushed me back out. Usually, I'd be stubborn and push my way back in. But, truthfully, I'm not too rushed to get back in there either.

I walk into the house, and the flicker of candlelight welcomes me home. The smell of fresh bread hits my nose, and Andi turns from the sizzling pot on the stove and smiles at me. I drop my lunchbox to the ground, and it hits with a thud.

"Hey, beautiful," I greet, fumbling to kick off my boots without untying them. I can't get to her fast enough. My hands slide on the silk of her pajamas as I wrap my arm around her waist and pull her into me.

She presses up on her toes to reach my face and places her supple, soft lips on mine. The spoon she was stirring the food with falls from her hand as I deepen the kiss. I swear I will show her exactly how much I love her every day for the rest of my life. Her tongue slips through my lips, and I run my hand down to her ass. She lifts her leg, and I hold it in place as she centers herself against my growing erection. She moans into my mouth, and the timer from the oven shrieks in the room.

"I've got to get the bread out," she pants, and I hang my head as I let her leg go. She giggles, but I'd rather have the house set on fire than stop kissing her.

She bounces to the oven mitt on the counter and pulls two loaves of bread from the oven.

"Damn, I'm one hell of a lucky man."

"It's my grandmother's recipe. Chicken and dumplings and warm homemade bread. Comfort food at its finest. You go get cleaned up, and I'll get the plates ready."

I give her a kiss, inhaling her sweet vanilla scent, and head back to the bedroom. By the time I get back, Andi has both TV trays set up in front of the couch.

"Perfect timing," she says as I take a seat next to her.

She flips on a home remodeling show on the TV. I take a bite of the chicken and dumplings and moan. "It's so good, babe. Thank you."

"You're welcome. Word to the wise, don't eat my mother's chicken and dumplings. They, um…how should I put this kindly. They aren't the same."

I laugh. "Noted."

"Speaking of my parents, they're coming into town tomorrow. They're going to stay at my house."

"Good. I'm glad they're coming. Are you going to stay there with them?"

"Do you want me to?" she asks, and I realize quickly how that may have come across.

I set my silverware down and turn to her. "You and I, we live together now. Whether that is here or there is solely up to you. As long as I'm with you, I'd live in a cardboard box next to the dumpster on the edge of town. If you want time alone with your parents, I will never stand in the way of that. But for the rest of our lives, I live where you live."

Her eyes drop, and I grab her hand. "I don't know when or if I'm going to feel happy in that house again. It's weird how easily that was taken away. But when I'm there, I can't help but remember the times I felt that creepy feeling. I'm hoping one day, the good memories will outweigh the bad ones."

"I understand. Then we just wait and see how each day goes."

"I love so much how you don't pressure me. It's just so easy with you, Mason."

"That's how it's supposed be, babe. I have a surprise for you." If she's going to stay here, I want her comfortable. This needs to feel like her home too. I get up from the couch, grab a card from my wallet, and sit back down next to her. "Here. Take my card and buy whatever you want to make this place your kind of cozy."

"Mason, you don't have to do this. I like it just the way it is."

"Uh-huh. I want matching blankets, but make mine a dark color, please."

A smile crosses her face. "You like my kind of cozy, don't you?"

"You've spoiled me, and now I want soft, fluffy shit all over my house. Don't tell Lucas."

She laughs, and my heart beats a little faster.

CHAPTER EIGHTEEN

Andi

MAMA PLACES A STACK of folded clothes into the dresser drawer. Her dark blue nail polish shines in the light that hangs above the guest bed. It took me forever to find the one I liked to go in here. I sit on the edge of the bed as she grabs the clothes from her suitcase, and the force with which she puts them away gets harder and harder with each stack.

"Mama?"

"You could have died, Andrea. What would I have done?" She puts her head in her hands. "We tried to get here as soon as we could."

"It's all right, Mama. We talked about this. I'm fine, and there was nothing you could have done."

"Thank God for Mason. If he wasn't here with you…" Her voice drops, and she shakes her head to gather herself.

I get up from the bed and hug her. Her signature scent that hasn't changed in at least thirty-five years hits my nose, and I feel a piece of home fill my heart. "Everything is okay. I just can't seem to shake this house."

"What do you mean?" she asks as I let her go and sit back down on the bed.

"The space just feels so violated. I'm having a hard time walking in here and remembering the smells of Grandma making snickerdoodles and apple pie." I laugh. "Remember how mad she used to get at the cat eating the tinsel off the Christmas tree? She'd be running after him yelling because he'd have a piece hanging out of his butt."

Mama laughs. "God, that was disgusting, wasn't it?"

I hold my stomach as the laughter stops. "But those memories feel so far away now. Now all I can think about is him watching me through the windows. I want to get over that. I just don't know how."

"Time, sweetheart. Time and new memories."

"I don't know how to make new memories if I don't even want to live here anymore."

"We'll talk about it more tomorrow. Tonight, we're going to get unpacked, and Daddy and I are going to relax. It was an emotional roller coaster for us until we actually got to hold you. I think tonight, we need to put our feet back on the ground."

"Is it weird for you guys to stay here by yourself? Do you want me to stay here with you?"

"Andrea. Your father grew up in this house. This house was part of us long before it was part of you. We're fine here. But you do whatever you need to."

She pats my shoulder and sighs. The clothes seem to have made peace with her again as she gently straightens them in the drawer.

"I've never seen Daddy hug a man like he hugged Mason." I thought I was going to have to pry Daddy off so Mason could breathe. It's safe to say Mason flew to the top of my daddy's list of favorite people.

"When you have kids, Andi, you'll understand. You never know if the person with your child is treating them the way you think they deserve to be treated. If they're good enough. If they love you enough. It's all scary. Mason proved himself, and I don't think Daddy or I will have those questions about him ever again."

"Kids? I don't know about that."

"I thought you always wanted kids, Andi," she says, holding her heart. "All your dolls had to get married and have kids. It was your dream. You don't want that anymore, sweetheart? It's fine if you don't. I'm just asking."

"I'm scared to go through it all again. I love Mason with my whole heart. But the thought of getting engaged is just as tainted as this house is now."

"First of all," she says, dropping her hand. The bed dips beside me as she sits with her hip against mine. "You don't have to get married to have kids. Second, can you honestly say Mason would do that to you?"

"This conversation is just too heavy for me right now."

"I'm sorry, honey. I get it. But you know I'm here to hold your hand through whatever you decide to do."

"I know, Mama."

———

MASON and I spent the day with Mama and Daddy. Mason took Daddy to the diner, and Mama and I had fun shopping for Mason's house. He told me to make it cozy, and that is right up my alley. Only I'm not going the light and airy route that I did with Grandma's house. I went to the little boutique in Birkenshire where I found my hand-knitted chunky blanket. Not only did they have another white one, they had a dark gray, which is perfect for Mason and my vision for his living room.

"I win," Daddy says, slamming down the last three cards in his hand.

"Why do we even bother playing this game with you?" I ask. Daddy has always been the king of rummy. Mason laughs, and Mama gathers the cards and puts them into the cardboard box. "Well, that was a fun day. I guess it's time to go." I pat Mason's leg, and he starts to get out of the kitchen chair.

"Hang on," Daddy says, holding his hand up. Mason relaxes back into the chair. "Your Mama and I want to talk to you about something," he says to me.

I eye Mama, and she's flinging the deck of cards into the drawer and biting her lip. "Oh God. You're scaring me." Mama sits down and interlocks her fingers.

"We have a proposal for you. But before we tell you what it is, we want to make sure you understand that there is zero pressure and it is completely your choice."

The desperation for water grows as I flick my eyes between my parents. "Just spit it out." Mason places his hand on my thigh and squeezes. Always here to calm me.

"We know this is still fresh for you, so don't make any rash decisions. Think it over first. But Mama and I have decided to move back to Cresna."

"Are you serious?" I shriek. "I've been begging you guys to move closer for so long. I can't believe this." I jump out of my chair and hug Mama.

"We travel so much anyway that the house in Wisconsin isn't doing anything for us anymore. We were trying to wait until a house came up on the market or some land."

"Wait," I say, holding my hand up. "What's the proposal?"

Daddy clears his throat. "It's just an idea, pumpkin. But Mama and I were thinking. What if we rented this house from you? It would still be yours. We'd just be living here for a while."

"And you'd make new memories in it with us. I'll host Christmas just like Grandma did. It wasn't even on our minds until you and I talked last night. I thought it could solve both of our problems. You need new memories, and we need to be closer to you," Mama says.

"Just think about it. We won't be upset at all if you hate the idea, and we'll wait for a house to come up," Daddy says.

I touch my fingertip to my bottom lip as a small pang of worry enters my body. "And I'd live…"

"Why are you even questioning this? You live with me," Mason says.

"Then no," I say, and all three faces fall. "I don't need time. This is where you two belong, and I need a fresh start."

The smile doesn't leave Mama's face as she hugs Mason and me goodbye. Daddy squeezes me tightly, then turns to Mason and says something in his ear that gets a smile. I wonder what he said as Mason grabs my hand, walks me out, and helps me into the car.

I never thought I'd move out of my grandmother's house. But it doesn't feel like I'm moving out because of negative emotions. It feels like I'm moving out because I'm moving in with the love of my life. My parents are going to be two streets away, which some people might hate but I can't wait for. Everything is falling into place, and as Mason pulls up to the little house on the edge of town, he reaches over and takes my hand.

"We're home, babe."

"My home is you. And there's no place else I'd rather be."

———

THE TWINKLING CHRISTMAS lights in the diner are so beautiful mixed with the soft amber glow from the new lights that hang above each table. I admire them for another moment, then head back into my office to wait for Tana and Brice to finish up with the closing tasks. Even after a few weeks, I couldn't bring myself to go back into the diner the way it was. All of Mason's friends chipped in to help, and within about six weeks, it was a brand-new place. My office was switched with the food stockroom, which ended up being much easier to access for the kitchen staff. And I have a brand-new office that has zero memories of Kenneth inside.

The soft cream walls are balanced with rich brown leather booths. The bright green plants that are scattered around the area bring a bit of airiness to the earthy tones. And with the big Christmas tree in the corner and the string lights hanging around the perimeter, this diner is one of the coziest places I love to be. It's only second to Mason's and my home, of course. Which is also fully decked out for the holiday.

I think everyone in town was a little nervous about coming back into the diner too. It took a few days for the regulars to start trickling back in. I'll never forget the first person at the door when I unlocked it two weeks ago today. Mr. Murphy marched inside, and without saying anything, he pulled me into his arms and hugged me. Then he patted my shoulder, gave me a kind smile, and took a seat in the closest booth to the door. He hasn't said one word to me about what happened. But that hug told me everything I needed to hear.

Tana walks into my office and leans against the walnut doorframe. "Brice asked if you bought three bags of that special black rice or four. Because he needs four for tomorrow's soup, but he can only find three."

Not this again. "I know I bought four."

"Well, he's in the kitchen having a breakdown because there's only three. Unless it got buried under something else. He couldn't find it though."

I roll my chair back as Tana's phone rings. She grabs it from her apron, looks at the screen, and gets a giddy look in her eye. "It's Lucas. I better tell him we're running late."

"You do that, and I'll go search the stockroom."

I've known Tana for a long time to know the smile that spread across her face as she answered the phone isn't her usual one. I bet she knows the gender of the baby, and I'm going to pull it out of her so help me. I only just found out Tana was pregnant a few weeks ago because they wanted to keep it to themselves for a little bit. After all of the loss they've been through, I'm sure they wanted to make sure everything was okay before sharing. All I know is those two are going to make one gorgeous baby.

I sigh as I head into the stockroom. Everything is organized into bins, plastic drawers, and shelves. I designed it to not only be functional but to look beautiful as well. The only problem is when something isn't in the right spot. The room was just replenished, and it's going to take me forever to go through this stuff. But happy staff means happy customers and a successful business. Not to mention they are more than just staff. The bond we have here at the diner is like nothing I've experienced working anywhere else. Tana has always been my partner when it comes to this place. But Brice has been the foundation of this restaurant for so many years. I thought I might lose him when I had to close for so long. But instead of leaving, he showed up every day with food to feed whoever was there working on the diner. That night changed us. All of us. I thought maybe Rhonda or Jessica would be too afraid to come back to work. But that didn't happen. The opposite did. They all rallied around me, helped get things back in order, and were standing right next to me when we reopened. That's what you do in a small town. We're family now.

I've sorted, moved, and rearranged so many things, and there's still no sign of that rice. The stockroom door opens, and Brice shouts in.

"I found it. I thought I only grabbed three, but there were four in my hand. My bad."

"Are you kidding me right now? I just spent twenty minutes searching for it."

"Sorry," he says, a wide grin on his face.

"Andi, can you come out here," Tana yells from the dining room. With the smile still plastered on his face, Brice holds the stockroom door open for me and nods toward the dining room. *What the hell is going on?*

Looking down the short hallway, the dining room is illuminated by only the Christmas lights. As the entire dining room comes into view, Mason stands in the middle of it, and he's all dressed up. The corner of his lips tip up, and he holds out his hand for me to go to him.

"What's all this?" I ask, running my eyes down his collared dress shirt, dark jeans, and his clean boots. I slide my hand into his and look up into his gorgeous speckled eyes.

"For so long, I convinced myself love didn't exist. True love. Not the kind of love that you only feel when you're right in front of someone. The kind that fills your whole heart, even when they aren't with you. I didn't think it was real because I never felt it for myself. I thought I did, but there is nothing that compares to how you make me feel. We've been through so many storms, and I'm sure there will be a few more in the future. Life isn't perfect. But I will always be your shelter from the rain."

My heart bangs against my chest, and I try to swallow as I remember the same words coming from my grandmother's mouth. The tears tickle my face as they fall.

Mason sinks to the ground on one knee. "Andrea Taylor, I have a question to ask you."

I hear a sniffle and the shuffling of many, many feet. I spin around to see all of our friends and family filing out of the kitchen and coming in through the front door. Daddy holds Mama as she wipes her nose with a napkin. Everyone that has a part in making my heart whole is in this room. Tana and Lucas. Owen and Natalie. Everest and Dani. Mr. Murphy, Brice, Rhonda, Jessica, and a photo of my grandma on the wall.

I turn back to Mason, my body surging with the love I have for him. Before I can say anything, he pulls a ring with a single round diamond from his pocket. "If you say yes, it's happening right now. I met you right here in this spot. This diner is part of you. It's part of me. This diner is us. And I want to marry you, right now. Here. Will you marry me, Andrea? Tonight?"

"Yes," I whisper. "Yes," I shout, bouncing up and down. The cheers and laughter fill the room as Mason slides the ring on my finger and jumps from the ground. I place my hand on his chest as he pulls me in close, and the heavy thuds of his heart hit my palm. He slides his hand into the side of my hair as he presses a long, deep, forever kind of kiss on my lips. Once our lips break, I wrap my arms around him and press my cheek to his. "We just have one little issue," I whisper in his ear.

"What's wrong?"

"We don't have a marriage license."

"I know. But we have an appointment tomorrow to get one," he whispers back. "So technically we won't be legally married until our commitment ceremony tomorrow. But tonight, we'll be married in our eyes and the eyes of our family and friends. We'll walk in tomorrow hand in hand, and there'll be no wondering. No worrying. Nothing but us. Together."

I sob as he speaks. He's thought of everything.

Mr. Murphy appears next to us with a bible in his hand. "Are you two ready?"

"Did you get ordained, Mr. Murphy?" I ask.

He nods. "Have been for years. I married your parents."

I turn to Mama, and she's a blubbering mess, and it makes me giggle. But even Daddy has a tear in his eye.

There is no other person in this entire world who knows me better or could love me more than Mason King. Tonight, I become Andrea King. And this is the wedding of my dreams.

EPILOGUE
SIX YEARS LATER

MASON

THE NOISE from inside Owen's house has Everest, Lucas, Owen, and me hiding outside. It's our favorite place to be when we're at the lodge. I wish I could bottle the smell of the tall pines and magnolias. But Andi and I come out often enough that I don't miss it for too long. Owen takes a drink from his beer, and Lucas grabs the last sprinkle donut from the box on the patio table.

"That's been sitting there all day," Everest says with disgust.

"So? There aren't any bugs on it, which means it's still good."

"Is there even any frosting left on it, or did it all melt off?" Owen asks, his face twisted.

Instead of answering, Lucas shoves the donut into his mouth and closes his eyes like it's the best donut he's ever eaten.

"You're disgusting," Everest says.

"I didn't have a choice," Lucas says. "Tana bet me we wouldn't finish off all the donuts we bought this morning. She said I got too many. Six years of marriage and she still doubts my abilities."

We all chuckle, knowing Lucas and Tana both love competition. Tana wins most of the time, but she should know better than to question Lucas and donuts.

"How's the Hilltop Lodge doing?" I ask Owen.

"Better than I could have expected. All my regulars love the new cabins and the stocked pond."

"It's got to be weird not having a bunch of people around all the time. Well, when we're not here anyway. I know the Hideaway Lodge was always booked solid," Everest says.

"It's perfect. The Hilltop is far enough away that Natalie and I have all the privacy we could dream of but close enough that I can get to it if there's any issues. It was the best decision we ever made."

"That's good to hear," Lucas says. "I was worried you'd regret closing down the Hideaway."

"The Hideaway isn't closed. It's just ours now. All of ours. I don't regret that for a fucking second."

Lucas and Tana have their own cabin that they built out here years ago. Everest and Dani used one of the original cabins that Owen built and added on additional rooms for their two children. Andi and I had to wait until our house in Cresna was finished being built before we could start on our new cabin at the Hideaway. It was finished just in time to bring our baby boy home from the hospital last year.

Other than the holidays we spend in Cresna with Andi's family at her grandmother's house, we celebrate every milestone at the Hideaway. All of us. With Lucas's two kids, Owen's three, Everest's two, and now my one, this place gets pretty damn loud when we're all together.

The sliding glass door opens, and Natalie steps out. "Break time's over, boys. It's time for cake, and then you're in charge of the kids because tonight is ladies' night down at the fire pit."

She rubs her hands together in excitement and then bounces

back in the house. "Well, brothers. We've been tagged in," Lucas says.

We rise from our seats and head inside, where chaos erupts. Everest's kids are at the table, coloring quietly. Lucas's kids are kicking a ball across the large living room and running after it screaming. Owen's son is in the corner with some kind of game system while his two daughters are playing on the floor. And my beautiful wife is snuggling our squealing boy in the kitchen. This is insanity. And I love every second of it.

"Okay, kids, time for cake!" Natalie calls in her sweet voice. But none of the kids move. "Kids, let's go. Time for cake," she repeats herself, but the kids are too loud in the big open space.

A whistle painfully hits my ear, and every kid freezes in place and looks at Everest.

"Table, now," he says, and all the kids rush to the table.

"Uncle Ever, you can whistle loud. I want to whistle loud," Iris says.

"I'll teach you after cake. But you have to promise not to do it in the house unless you're right next to Pops." I laugh as I overhear their conversation. Iris started calling Lucas Pops shortly after Lucas and Tana got married. It was one of the few times I saw Lucas get emotional. Pops fits him so well, and all of his kids call him that now.

As we all crowd around the dining room table in Owen and Natalie's house, singing happy birthday to their two-year-old daughter, I watch Andi on the other side of the room. Her arm is interlocked with Tana's as she laughs at something Natalie said, and her natural shine nearly blinds me. How did I get so lucky? How do I deserve this? Those are questions I'll probably never know the real answer to. I'm pretty sure none of us truly deserve the women we've had the privilege to fall in love with.

Out of the corner of my eye, Starling's foot slips off the chair she's standing on just out of reach of all of us, and she falls to the ground. Four men rush to her, but Owen gets there first and picks her up. We huddle around her, making sure she's okay as she cries. Natalie pushes through the mass of men who have all melted into a big puddle at the sight of one of our kids hurt.

"Let me see her," she says, reaching for Starling. She looks her over and rolls her eyes. "She's fine, you guys. Calm down."

There is no such thing as calm down when it comes to our kids. Any of them. We're protective of all of them as if they were all our own. Iris is already ten years old, and I can tell with her gorgeous blonde hair, the boys are going to be chasing her. I almost feel bad for the boys though. Because we'll be chasing them.

A few hours later, our wives have abandoned us. They went down to the fire pit in the grassy area by the lodge and brought a whole lot of wine in their arms. I'm assuming we'll each be carrying our wife to our cabins tonight.

I never thought I'd be jealous of a room full of kids, but I never got to have sleepovers like they do when we come here. I don't know how Natalie and Owen do it. They love having all these children in the house, and they set up the entire loft as one huge pallet of blankets and pillows for the kids. They have a blast. And every morning, Natalie will make breakfast, and Lucas will go get donuts from his favorite donut shop.

The kids are all tucked in, though it will probably be at least another hour before they stop giggling and whispering enough to fall asleep. Owen walks out of the kitchen with three beers and a soda in his hands. He hands me and Lucas a beer and Everest the soda. He plops down on the couch and takes a drink of his.

"I thought it was your turn tonight," Everest says to Owen.

"Nope, I did it last time. Definitely your turn," Owen says back. We all laugh because we have the same conversation every time we're in charge of the kids. One of us doesn't drink in case there's an emergency and someone needs to drive. It's how we're wired. Always thinking two steps ahead and keeping our loved ones safe.

Lucas talks about roofing, Owen talks about Hilltop, Everest talks about the next house they're flipping, and I talk about the diner, each of us filled with so much pride because of our accomplishments. Before long, the noise from upstairs stops, and we relax down into the couches in Owen's living room.

Everest chuckles.

"What's so funny?" Lucas asks.

"Us. Who would have thought this is where the four of us would be? Am I the only one who sits and thinks about that sometimes?"

"No, brother," Owen says. "I think about it all the time. I really think I might not have been here today if it wasn't for you guys."

"What is this? Sappy hour at the Hideaway? God, you guys are really bringing down the mood," Lucas says.

"What mood?" I ask. "It's a Friday night, and we're sitting at home with our kids while our wives party down at the fire. There is no mood here."

We all scrunch up our faces as we laugh, trying not to wake up the kids.

"Seriously though," Everest says. "Look at us. We're not perfect, but we fought our asses off to get here. We managed to land on our feet. I'm fucking proud of us."

Everest reaches out his soda bottle, and we all hold our beers in the center of our circle.

"We've been through a lot," I say. "Life threw us out of a plane with no parachute. But I think we all landed exactly where we were supposed to be. Together. Family. Brothers for life."

ACKNOWLEDGMENTS

I don't put acknowledgements in all of my books, but my gratitude and love is steadfast through every single word that is published. So much goes into writing, editing, proofing, and publishing each book, and I could never do it alone.

I have to give my first and biggest thanks to my husband. Without him, I wouldn't be able to do this. When I first said I wanted to write a book, he didn't laugh. He didn't make that funny "humpf" sound some people do when they think you're nuts. He also didn't say one word when I told him how much it was going to cost to put out my first book. Instead, he looked me in the eye and told me to go for it (like he does with everything). He's amazing for so many reasons, and he works his ass off so I can do this. *I love you, babe.*

To my kids. Thank you for giving Mama her writing time. I know it's hard sometimes for you when I'm working, but even when I'm in the middle of writing a big scene, I'll never forget the little knocks on my door for a hug or kiss. Thank you for those, because sometimes, I really need them. You're my favorite boy and girl in the whole wide world. I love you both so much.

There aren't enough words to thank my alpha-beta reader, Tracey Wilson-Vuolo. You are my rock, my cheerleader, and my treasured friend. I'd be completely lost without you. Thank you so much for everything you do, Tracey. I love you so much. (Even if you hate all my name ideas.)

To my alpha-beta reader Elaine Hennig. You are an absolute rock star. Your attention to detail is impeccable, and you make me look at things from an entirely different perspective. Our conversations keep me laughing, and your wise words of advice keep me grounded. I'm beyond thankful to have you in my life. Thank you so much! I love you, friend!

To my readers. None of this would be possible without you. I got this calling one day to write the story that had been swirling in my head for over a year. To be honest, I didn't think I could do it. I sat down and thought, *If I could just write one chapter...* Well, one chapter turned into two. Then three and so on. When that book was finished, I had never been more proud of myself in my life. Then I realized I was going to have to let other people read it too. And that was scary. If I had known you all were out there, I wouldn't have been afraid. I'm so grateful that you read and love my stories because I write them for you. I wish I could hug every one of you for making my dreams come true. Thank you so much.

To all the bloggers. I can't express how happy you all make me. Thank you for all the shares, likes, and comments. I'm aware of the time it takes to read and review books and that there are hundreds of them out there. I hope you know how much I appreciate and respect your time. Thank you for being so wonderful to me.

To my editor, Sandra. Girl, you save my ASS! I would be up a creek without a paddle. I'd have peanut butter but no jelly. I'd have coffee but no cream (sacrilege!)! I couldn't publish anything without your help! You are one of the hardest workers I know. I hope one day you get the rest you deserve! You are an incredible woman, and I'm so lucky to even know you. Thank you for all you do. So much love for you.

PREVIEW OF LIBBY LANE
CHAPTER ONE

Cora

The light, rhythmic thud of my running shoes hitting the dirt path is a sound I've become addicted to. I could run this trail with my eyes closed. Every curve and turn is etched into my memory. Living in Jasper Creek my whole life, I've played in these woods since I could walk. At the end of Libby Lane, there's a path that winds through this wooded area behind the town.

About a half mile in, you'll find the big pond. It's Jasper Creek's best-kept secret. Most of my teenage years were spent jumping into the water from the rope swing that hangs from the big crooked tree branch. But now, hardly anyone comes back here. Instead of kids riding bikes, playing ball in the park, or spending the summer swimming at the pond, they're playing video games or on their phone. It's sad really. Then again, the woods have kind of become the place I come to get away.

It's easy to forget the monotony of life when I'm out here. The wind blows the small pieces of hair that have fallen out of my high pony and cools the sweat from the Kentucky summer heat. I inhale deeply through my nose, tilt my head back, and watch the glimmer of the setting sun on the tops of the trees. Slowing my pace to a slow walk, I close my eyes and breathe deeply to cool down. This is my favorite part of my routine. When it's just me and the sound of the leaves being played by the wind right after a good run and any frustrations I may have had are gone. It's the moment of peace. Just before I open my eyes again, something throws off my balance. My ankle twists and I fall to the ground with a thud. *Shit.*

Turning my head I look for the damn stick that ruined my tranquility and tripped me. There's no stick. The tail end of a snake slithers off the path and into the trees. Adrenaline rushes through my body like a rocket at the same time a scream so high-pitched I didn't even know that tone could come out of me echoes against the tree trunks. I push myself off the ground and attempt to get as far away from the area as I can. All I know is it was long, slithery, and brown. I don't know the difference between poisonous and non-poisonous snakes. Not like I really give a shit either way. I've had a fear of snakes ever since my brother decided to scare me with one when I was little. I've always cried when I get really scared. This time is no exception, and the uncontrollable tears flood my eyes. The terror has taken over. The only thing I can think about is getting the hell out of these woods.

I push through the pain in my ankle and begin hobbling as quickly as I can go down the path. I keep a constant watch behind me. Realistically, I know that snake isn't chasing after me. But that isn't the side I'm listening to right now. The irrational side has taken over my brain and is screaming at me that the snake from hell is hunting me down and is going to eat me whole. Then something else scares me even more. I run into something tall and hard. *Please be a tree. Please be a tree.* My head tips back slowly, and my eyes travel up as my heart sinks. I didn't run into a tree. I ran into a man. One I don't know. That doesn't happen in Jasper Creek. I know everyone.

His beautiful gray eyes hit mine, and for a split second,

neither of us say a word. "Are you okay?" he asks, snapping out of our eye lock. He grabs my arm and pulls my body behind his as he looks down the path where I just came from. I try to speak, but I'm so out of breath nothing comes out. "Is someone chasing you?" His voice is so deep it reverberates in my ears.

"No," I blurt out finally. "I stepped..." I take a breath in. "On a..." Another. "A fucking snake." My body shivers as I say it out loud.

"A snake?" His body relaxes and he drops his other hand that I now realize had been rested on the butt of his gun. Bored. His expression turns bored. "That's what you screamed like a maniac about?"

As I back away from him, I take in the marvelous view that stands in front of me. The sleeves on his shirt are a tight fit around his arms. The black pants and shiny black shoes all match his black tactical belt. *Shit.* He's the new cop that moved in down the street that everyone has been talking about. No one in town has met him yet, but there isn't anything good being said about him. All we know is that he was a police officer in Atlanta before taking a job at Holland City Police Department. However, I don't think anyone has actually laid their eyes on him. If they did, there'd be something good to say. *Hot damn.* I bring my vision back to his face that is now slightly tilted to the side with one eyebrow cocked. His bulky forearms are now crossed, and he's waiting for an answer.

"Have you ever stepped on a snake before?" I ask.

"No."

"Well, maybe if you did, you'd scream like a little girl. You don't know."

"That would never happen. I don't get scared. Besides, I tend to watch where I'm walking."

The arrogance that surrounds his words makes me want to

punch him in the nose. He might be able to talk to a lady like that where he comes from, but around here respect is expected.

"Listen…" I no sooner get the first word of my soon-to-be lecture out when I forget about my ankle and step on it. Through my gritted teeth, I hiss and his arm shoots out and around my waist. He stops me from falling, and before I know what's happening, he picks me up and begins carrying me. I'm in good shape, but I'm a curvy woman. There's only a few men I know that could swipe me up like he just did. His long stride is probably three strides for my short legs, but he's also walking fast. For a second, I have a lapse in control and take a long, deep whiff of the leather musk coming from his neck. Only a second though.

"Put me down."

"What's your name?" he asks, ignoring my demand.

"Excuse me, but I requested to be put down."

"Name."

Tired of his cold tone and lack of manners, I refuse to give him an answer. "Unless you are asking as a police officer, it's none of your business. Now put. Me. Down."

With quick movements, he swings me upright but carefully places me back on my feet. Once I'm steady, he lets go, then without saying a word, walks away. My hands rest on my hips, and I huff out loud at the rudeness that just transpired. We aren't that far from the road, so I lose sight of him rather quickly. Part of me is surprised that he just walked away like that. I asked to be put down, not abandoned. *Asshole.*

Carefully, I put a little weight on the ball of my foot and begin limping down the path. I wish I could say that my mother's grace was passed down to me. It wasn't. I've become pretty knowledgeable of the telltale signs of broken bones. My guess is it's just a sprain, which is still a pain in my ass. Knowing I have a little ways to go, I try to hop on one foot to take some of the pressure off but only get a few feet before I start to hobble again.

Frustrated, I grunt from deep within my throat. This is just like me. So stubborn. I could've already been home by now had I just put up with rude cop guy. Irritation starts to build within me. I'm angry that I'm hurt. My peaceful moment of the day was perfect and then *boom!* Snake and a jerk face. I mock his cocky facial expressions when my impressions get interrupted. My body catapults off the ground once more.

"Can't take watching you struggle. I'm carrying you home. Don't argue. Won't work this time."

"Did you just come from behind me?"

He nods. "You honestly think I would leave you alone and injured in the woods?"

"I guess you're not the asshole I thought you were."

"I didn't say that. Truth is, I just want a shower and a cold beer. I can't do that while you're still out here."

"Wow. That charm of yours must have helped you get all the ladies' digits."

His condescending smirk just irritates me more. I've been so focused on his snotty attitude and not where we are that I didn't even notice that we made it out of the woods already. He walks us up to the old Montgomery house. I remember Mr. Montgomery from when I was a child. He was an old grump. Must be the house.

Rude cop guy places me down on the top step, then moves around me. The sound of keys jingle in my ear as he lets himself in the house. Through the screen door he says, "Stay there."

My mouth opens, but he walks out of sight before anything can come out. *Fuck this.* I'm not staying here. I'm not a damn dog he can order around. I've limped halfway down his driveway before I suddenly feel myself lifted off the ground again. He brings me back to the steps, sets me down, then puts a bag of frozen peas on my ankle.

"You need ice and to stay off of it. But from what I've seen, you don't really listen to instructions well."

"I don't respond to commands. Especially not from strange men who just moved here and apparently don't know the proper way to treat a lady."

He takes a deep breath and blows it out forcefully while rubbing his face. "Well, we wouldn't be strangers had you told me your name now, would we?"

Maybe I missed the exhaustion in his face when we were in the woods. Or maybe he's just now letting it show. But the black circles under his eyes don't lie. Shoulders that were strong and broad in the woods are now angled toward the ground, his muscles relaxed. We may have gotten off to a rough start, but the man did just carry me for about a half mile.

"Cora," I say quietly.

"What?"

"My name is Cora," I yell out of spite. He rolls his eyes but can't hide the smirk. "Well, it's CoraLynn, but nobody calls me that other than my mama and Mae."

"Wyatt."

"Can I ask you somethin', Wyatt?" He nods, tucking his thumbs into the top of his duty belt. "How come you've been here for a few weeks but nobody's even met you yet?"

"Started on night shift and slept during the day. Today's my second day working day shift. It sucks and I'm tired."

I giggle. "That's far from rumors that have been swirling around town."

"Good stuff, huh?"

"There is." Not wanting to elaborate further on that, I look to the west and see the sun has set. It's getting dark. "Then again, from our experience today, I'd guess half of it is probably right." Rising from the step, I stand and brush off the dirt that's still stuck to my ass from falling.

He pushes off the front porch pillar that he was leaning against and digs in his pocket, coming out with his keys again.

"I'll drive you home."

"That's really unnecessary. I just live…"

An annoyed grin appears on his face, and he leans down close to me. "Are we really going to continue this game?"

He thinks I'm playing a game? Fine. "Okay then. Drive me home, Officer." I smile sarcastically, and he looks intrigued but doesn't question.

Wyatt's arm wraps around my waist, and his fingers hold strong to my hip. *God he smells good.* He gives me more help than I probably need to walk around the car and into the passenger seat of his black Dodge Charger. I hold it together as I watch him jog back to the driver's side. I stifle my giggle as the engine purrs to life. I don't laugh as he backs out, puts it in drive, and presses on the gas.

"Right there." My voice cracks as I try to hold in my laughter.

"What?"

"My house is right there. The second driveway on the right."

As he pulls into my driveway two houses down from his, I no longer hold it together. My laughter fills the car. "For a cop, you really suck at observation." I open the passenger door as he reaches for his handle. "I promise you, I don't need any more help today. But thank you."

"Have you always been this stubborn?" he asks.

Memories of years ago flood into the forefront of my brain. Memories from back when I knew nothing of the turmoil life could bring. I can feel the smile disappear from my face, and I look to a flower that's hanging upside down from his rearview mirror.

"No," I say quietly. Movement from the driver's seat snaps me out of my daze, and I flash him a quick half smile, then hop out of his car.

————

"Dammit!" The words come out louder than I thought they would.

After Wyatt dropped me off an hour ago, I grabbed the bowl of pasta salad out of the fridge, poured myself a glass of sweet tea, and headed to my favorite spot in the house. Titus built the porch swing for me last year right after I moved in. It's where I spend most of my nights. My feet draped over the custom center console, with a light blanket over my legs is my usual position out here. I stand up, ready to head inside for the night when I place too much weight on my sore ankle. I drop everything in my hands in order to stop myself from falling again. I think for sure I'll see Mae's lights go on from the ruckus. She lives on the next street, but from my front porch you can see the back of her house between the yards. She must have gone to bed early tonight. Carefully, I kneel down and gather the pieces of glass that have strewn about my porch from my mason jar of tea. It must have hit the ground just right for it to break like this.

"Cora?" A deep voice from the dark startles me. If I hadn't already been on the floor, I would have been from the jolt of hearing my name come out of the silence of night.

I straighten my back to peer over the half wall that goes around my porch. Wyatt is running up my yard in jeans with no shoes. No shirt either. The closer he gets, the further my mouth opens. His fit torso twists with every pump of his arms. "Cora?" he calls again.

"Stop!" I whisper as he reaches the second step up to the porch. "There's glass."

He ignores my warning and continues up the stairs. Without saying a word, he places his hands under my armpits, lifting me straight off the ground, and places me back on the swing.

"The glass…"

"I told you. I watch where I step." His eyes glare at me with concern. I smile at his smart-ass answer, and a surprising matching grin shows up on his face. "Do you have a broom?"

"In the kitchen. I'll…"

"You'll stay right there. Where is it?"

"Kitchen. Pantry door is open on the right."

He disappears for only a minute before coming back out with the broom. The fact that I still think he's an ass doesn't change the fact that he is sexy to watch sweep my front porch. With each swipe of the broom, the muscles in his arms pulse, and all I'm thinking about is what else I can throw on the floor for him to sweep. I'm caught off guard when I snap out of it and see him squinting at me. *Great.* More reason for his head to expand with his ego. In an attempt to quit staring, I resume my normal position on the swing and look out onto Libby Lane.

"Damn," he says. The broom falls to the floor, and Wyatt walks over the pile of dirt and glass to me. The palm of his hand cups my calf as he pulls my ankle close to his face. "I don't like that." *Oh, but I do.* His fingertips gently graze the lower half of my leg. *Dear sweet Jesus.* It's been over a year since a man put his hands on me. Now rude cop guy is on his knees in front of me with no shirt on, and his gentle fingers are traipsing over my skin. This is like dangling a big piece of chocolate cake in front someone on a diet. I fucking love cake.

"It's fine. I'm sure it's just a sprain."

Wyatt shakes his head, removes his hands from my leg, and goes back to sweeping the bits of glass into the pan.

"If that's broken and you ignore it, it either won't heal at all or it won't heal right. Then you'll have to hobble around for the rest of your life, and I'll tell you I told you so."

"I'm so glad you came over. You should really come back tomorrow. I'm not sure what I'll do without your negativity cluttering up my blue skies."

With his face still angled to the porch floor, I almost missed his silent chuckle. He turns with the dustpan full of glass shards toward the front door. The light from the kitchen shines just enough for me to catch his eyes as they flick to me before disappearing inside. They burned. The way his eyes looked at me felt like fire on a hundred-degree night. *So fucking hot.* I'm not sure how to take this guy. He seems like he's incredibly annoyed by me on one hand. But on the other, the way his fingers ran across my skin was...*Oh God.* He was only half checking that bruise. I can't help but close my eyes thinking about the way his touch felt and where else I wish he'd touch me. The screen door slams, causing me to jump, and my eyes fly open. Wyatt is staring at me, and I'm not sure how long he's been there. The corners of his mouth turn up in an evil grin. I realize that my bottom lip has been sucked inside my mouth and is being held there by my teeth as my eyes are closed, dreaming about hot, steamy rude cop guy.

Wary of my foot sitting across the center console of my porch swing, he blows out a long exhale and sits down on the other side. Usually the breeze gently sways the swing, and I love the sound of the chains as they squeak slowly. That's not happening right now though. Wyatt is aggressively pushing the swing back and forth at a speed not meant for these chains. After watching him for a minute, I realize that he rarely is still as his fingers play with the chain, then rub the armrest. He continuously looks around, as if he's making note of every sound. I don't think this guy knows how to relax.

"Slow down," I say.

"What?"

"Slow. Down. You're giving me whiplash."

Both of his feet hit the floor and the swing suddenly stops before beginning to move again at a slower pace. I let a few minutes of silence pass before I can't take it anymore.

"So...Wyatt...what brought you to Jasper Creek?"

He moves his hand over his dark brown hair and gets up from the swing.

"You good?" he asks, standing next to the stairs.

I guess we're done talking. "I'm good."

With a quick nod, he jogs down the stairs and across the street. Between the moonlight and the glow from the streetlamp, the muscles on his back are highlighted with each pump of his arms. What a weird day. It doesn't sit well with me that Wyatt doesn't want to talk about why he came to Jasper Creek. Maybe it's nothing and I'm thinking way too far into it. Or, maybe he has something to hide.

Libby Lane is available now!

ALSO BY C.E. JOHNSON

Elements of the Heart Series

Watch Me Drown

Watch Me Burn

Watch Me Breathe

Watch Me Land

In the Dark Series

Done

Just One

Buried Hearts

Jasper Creek Series

Libby Lane

Standalone

Rain

ABOUT THE AUTHOR

C.E. Johnson writes contemporary romance with a dash of suspense. Her stories are full of emotion, heartbreak, collapsing walls, and redeeming love.

When not writing until all hours of the night, she loves to read stories that rip your heart out completely, then kindly place it back into your chest with a HEA.

She lives in the Midwest with her husband, two kids, and some spoiled rotten animals.

Learn more about C.E. Johnson and her books at:
AuthorCEJohnson.com

Want to know all about C.E's releases, exclusive teasers, and lots of fun?
Join C.E.'s Reading Roses reader group on Facebook!

Made in the USA
Coppell, TX
15 April 2022

76635576R00121